THE SUBMERGED

Winner of the Flannery O'Connor Award for Short Fiction

The University of Georgia Press Athens

Will Boast

THE SUBMERGED

stories

The author thanks the publications in which these stories first appeared: "The Barber of Erice" in *The American Scholar* (Winter 2025), *The Comma Press* (Sept. 2024), and on BBC Radio 4 (audio; Sept. 2024); "The Submerged" in *The American Scholar* (Winter 2021); "In the Leaves" in *The Southern Review* (Autumn 2006); "The Human Conditional" in *Switchyard* (Winter 2025); "Weather Enough" in *The Mississippi Review* (Autumn 2007) and *Best New American Voices 2009*; "At the Center of the Sailing World" in *Narrative* (April 2011); "Flight of the Dodo" in *ZYZZYVA* (Summer 2024); "Black Car" in *Granta* (Oct. 23, 2019); and "Decoys" in *ZYZZYVA*.

Published by the University of Georgia Press
Athens, Georgia 30602
www.ugapress.org

Designed by Mindy Basinger Hill
Set in Garamond Premier Pro
Printed and bound by Sheridan Books
The paper in this book meets the guidelines for permanence and durability of the Committee on Production Guidelines for Book Longevity of the Council on Library Resources.

Printed in the United States of America

30 29 28 27 26 P 5 4 3 2 1

EU Authorized Representative
Easy Access System Europe—Mustamäe tee 50, 10621 Tallinn, Estonia, gpsr.requests@easproject.com

Library of Congress Control Number: 2026938941
ISBN: 9780820377865 (paperback)
ISBN: 9780820377872 (epub)
ISBN: 9780820377889 (PDF)

FOR AJB, RJB, AND NPB *yours and yours and yours*

CONTENTS

THE SUBMERGED

THE BARBER OF ERICE

It started with the most miraculous haircut Giuliu had ever seen.

Signora Azzaro had brought in her thirteen-year-old son. Every boy in Erice wanted to look like a footballer, but this . . . The sides had been brought down to nearly stubble, then textured in tight zigzags like lightning bolts. The top had been made to stand at attention, somewhere between a mohawk and a pompadour, except the front, which swept moodily down over the boy's eyes. In the back, above a delicately faded neckline, were two more bolts, larger, but done with absolute precision. There were even, Giuliu saw as he sat the boy in the second chair, notches carved out of his slender eyebrows, also, impossibly, in the shape of lightning.

"Mizzica," Giuliu muttered. "Where did you go for this?"

Signora Azzaro threw up her hands. "Two weeks from his confirmation, and he looks like some Catania gangster. You can fix it, can't you?"

"A salon in Trapani maybe?" But that was all the way down the mountain, never mind that no one he knew of in Trapani was even capable of such work.

"He doesn't tell me," Signora Azzaro answered bitterly. "Just says a friend did it."

Giuliu swept the pompadour one way, then the other, considering. Perhaps there was some way to fix it, but Giuliu had the long-dulled instincts of a man with a captive clientele. He'd cut this boy, and all the boys and men in Erice, so many times that their hair was just an eternal weed to be pruned and pruned. As the clippers whirred, the boy scowled back at him in the mirror. Faint traces of lightning could still be seen, and short of shaving them off, he couldn't do much about the eyebrows. "There we are," Giuliu said. "Now he only looks like a Napoli gangster."

Signora Azzaro cuffed her son on the ear. "This is the impression we give Padre Barale?"

Giuliu couldn't hide his irritation at the mention of the handsome new priest. "Don't worry. Barale's too busy with his good works to worry how the flock gets shorn."

"Yes, yes"—Signora Azzaro counted out exactly six euros—"for your efforts."

Giuliu swept up, dipped his combs, counted the register back out, as if there'd been any other customers that day. He felt the usual low hum of panic—his shop, his father's shop, going down the toilet. But, as he closed up, there was something else: remorse. All of that beautiful work, disappearing under his clippers.

Just once in your life, the guidebook said, you must see the sun set over Erice.

Giuliu sat in the piazza watching a clutch of tourists snap the same photo—the blood-orange sun trembling into the Tyrrhenian Sea, the Isole Egadi slanting mile-long shadows up the mountain, the whole burning sky going ruddy-dark red as the day bled out in the bath—that every other grinning idiot off the cruise liners had taken for the past forty years. Or, anyway, ever since Giuliu was a boy. Even the sublime grows a rind.

He poured himself another grappa as the rest of the village straggled by: The elderly couples hobbling through their passeggiata. The mothers herding their little ones toward Wednesday mass. Father Barale smiling beatifically as he crossed the square, stopping to juggle a football with some boys. In the café next to Giuliu's shop, the usual clutch of old codgers sat playing scopa and grousing over their amari, while the proprietor gazed hopefully at the tourists, who, satisfied with their photos, trailed off toward their waiting coach. You must see the sun set over Erice, the guidebook said, but save your appetite till you get back to your cruise.

Through the haze of dusk and grappa, Giuliu noticed that the boys playing football looked freshly cut. He couldn't remember when he'd last seen some of them in the shop. But something else caught his gaze: a tall, rawboned African rushing over to the departing tourists—"My friends! Where you come from?"—with cheap handicrafts.

"Che palle!" a voice called out. Giuliu turned to see Marco arriving. "They'll drive away all our visitors! Then where will we be, Giu? No one comes to Sicily to buy little drums."

"He hauled all that crap up here," Giuliu said. "Give him that."

"Dai! The government gives them free bus passes. Don't be so naïve."

"Right," Giuliu answered quickly, "and we pay for them!" Maybe if it were Syrians coming here, he went on, but all these Algerians and Senegalese? They were just after work, flooding in because Brussels and Berlin had thrown the doors open. Maybe they could afford to be generous up north, but Sicily was poor, Erice even poorer. "Yet we're expected to take in all these blacks and panhandlers? Cazzo!" Giuliu looked over at his friend for approval.

Since age three, Marco had been his constant companion. They'd chased all over the mountain, spinning out fantasies of adventure and escape, chubby, wheezy Giuliu always two steps behind Marco, who'd started wearing a mustache in scuola media. Now they sat scorning Erice's decay, striking roguish poses but ever closer to becoming those old farts in the café. Marco wore his Enel uniform—he read meters all across the province—his utility bag still slung over his shoulder as he glowered at the African. Experimentally, Giuliu also called out, "Che palle!"

Marco socked Giuliu in the arm. "Watch your language, eh? There are children here."

Giuliu shrank in embarrassment and confusion. But a moment later, Marco pulled a second bottle of grappa from his bag and, pouring them both a glass, raised a mock toast to the passing elders. "To our noble Christian Democrats, long be their last days in the sun!"

"To Brussels!" Giuliu added. "Long may they tax our asses blue!"

Marco roared with laughter, then broke out in song. "Ah, che bel vivere, che bel piacere per un barbiere di qualità!"

Feeling woozy and flush, Giuliu joined in for a few bars. But his attention was dragged away again by the lanky African, who'd given up on the tourists and was now kicking the football around with the boys while the mothers looked on warily.

"Sto stronzo," Marco muttered.

Giuliu was about to agree. But just then an errant kick came their way. The African ran over to retrieve the ball, and as he turned back around, Giuliu saw it, as sharp as a slap to the face: trimmed out of the guy's fade, one on each side, two perfectly shaped lightning bolts.

The next afternoon, Giuliu closed early—he'd done little save sharpen his shears—and marched down the winding footpath to the old convent and rectory. He came into the grove, where the two cloistered buildings sat in tranquil shambles. The dense, daydream scent of jasmine hung on the breeze, and ochre sunlight stippled the soft carpet of leaves, such that Diana herself might step out of the trees. But Giuliu marched straight ahead, in no mood to admire the day.

Following a clutter of voices, he came into the courtyard and saw a milling crowd of about sixty, all Africans and Arabs. Bristling, he went quickly on to the rectory. Two years ago, Barale had arrived—replacing a miserable Capuchin who had dropped dead in the middle of Epiphany—and set about converting the disused convent into a camp for refugees and other layabouts. Till recently, they hadn't been seen much in the village, preferring to pester the tourists down in Trapani. Well, Giuliu wouldn't stand for them taking over Erice too. Just as he was about to hammer on the rectory door, however, he heard a familiar sound. He followed the electric, insect whine back to the courtyard. And there, in the center of a loose circle of men, stood the source of his outrage and worry.

At a makeshift barber station—cracked picture-frame mirror propped on a chair, red plastic bucket for a sink—a slight, very dark-skinned man wielded the buzzing clippers. He wore baggy trousers and a faded red polo, while the others were in shorts, jeans, and Manchester United and Barcelona jerseys, cheap knockoffs that made them look even more foreign. But their hairstyles . . . High fades, drop fades, braids set off with zigzags, hard parts, platinum-dyed tips, textured falling quiffs . . . Even the most flamboyant striker would have trouble maintaining such looks. The short man was cutting a Middle Eastern guy, holding the clippers at a strange angle but working with total focus. Giuliu squinted and leaned forward, so entranced that he jumped at a voice behind him.

"Welcome, Signore Rizzuto."

"Father Barale," Giuliu said coolly.

"And how are you enjoying this fine afternoon? I confess I'm still unaccustomed to the beauty of this place. To have known it your whole life!"

Giuliu, bridling at the priest's smile, said only, "Your man over there is killing me."

"Sorry?" The priest ran a hand through his hair, giving himself away. "Oh, you mean Baba? In the red shirt?"

"Our boys, Erice's boys," Giuliu said gravely, "are coming here to get cut."

"Our doors are open," the priest said. "This isn't a prison. And I suppose it could even be, well, something of an intercultural experience."

"Yes, yes, very lovely. Except your Babbo, or whoever, is filching my customers. How do you think I make my living? As meagre as it is."

The priest nodded slowly, radiating contemplation as if he were Solomon himself.

"It isn't safe," Giuliu put in. He wasn't sure quite what he meant, so he added, "You need a license to be a barber in this country." He gestured toward the courtyard. "This is . . . unhygienic."

The priest sighed. "I'd pay our guests to fix up the facilities, give them a bit of pocket money. But we're at a deficit already."

"Look, your Babbo can cut his friends here. But I'll have to draw the line at our boys. After all, we wouldn't want the Ministry of Health involved."

Barale suddenly brightened, as if he'd scarcely heard the threat. "There's an idea! Why don't you hire Baba?"

Giuliu nearly spit in the dirt. "But he, I . . . you couldn't possibly—"

"Take him on as your apprentice. We're eager for any of these men to have work, proper work. You'd be doing the community a great service."

"The community?! Look here, Father, we're not all aiming for sainthood. Keep our boys from coming down here, or I'll inform the authorities."

Barale spread out his arms, about to ascend that very moment. "I understand your caution, Signore Rizzuto. But—" He seemed to reconsider, tugging again on his shaggy hair. "Well, perhaps I'll have to come see you, and we can discuss it further."

Scoffing, Giuliu waved again at the courtyard—"Why don't you have him do it? He'll give you a cut worthy of Balotelli himself"—then, in a huff, set off back up the path.

He read the *Giornale* front to back, dipped and redipped his combs, went through his bills, most of them second or third notices, reorganized his supply closet, then meticulously oiled the levers on both his chair and the first chair, the one his father had used. Giuliu had grown up in the shop, a heady male world of cigar smoke, rude jokes, and the old ballads his father and the customers often broke into. Some mornings, Giuliu came down to the shop and it all seemed to be still hanging in the air. As for his mother, she'd fled Erice when he was four, all the way to Milano, where, village gossip had it, she'd married some big wheel at the stock exchange. He'd always thought he'd go off to find her, one of his many stifled fancies. When he was eighteen, his father died of lung cancer—and suddenly, with scarcely the chance to plan any other avenue through life, Giuliu himself became the barber of Erice.

He was reclining in the second chair, puzzling over a classified in the *Giornale*—"Stairs for sale, Christ just take them, they're not going anywhere"—when the bells on the door rang out. He heaved himself up, glad at least for some business. Then he saw who it was.

"So," he said, "Barale sent you instead."

Up close, Giuliu could see that the man was around forty, at least as old as himself. He was balding, a little hunched, and stood with his hands clasped behind his back, a quizzical look furrowing his brow. "Hello, yes, you are the one named Giulio?" His Italian was jumpily enunciated but surprisingly competent.

"Giuliu," he answered drily. "Like my papa before me."

"My sincere apologies, Mr. Giuliu. Now I would just like to introduce myself. I am Boubacar Condeh. Baba, for short. I am very sorry to disturb you today, sir."

"Yes, well, you've caught me at a free moment." Giuliu cleared his throat. "Look, sorry to disappoint you and his holiness, but I'm not looking for apprentices."

"That is not the reason for my visit, sir. I understand that we may have a disagreement. But today I am here to ask you a favor."

He took from behind his back something wrapped in cloth. For a moment, Giuliu thought he was going to be robbed. Then he saw that it was a pair of shears.

"I am asking if you are able to sharpen these."

Find someone in Trapani, Giuliu was about to say. Or, better yet, mail them away, far away. Then he saw the condition of the blades, the chips in their edges, the dulled luster of the steel. "Bedda Matri! What have you been using on these?"

"Padre Barale provided a knife sharpener from the kitchen, but I do believe that—"

"From the kitchen?! Cazzo. Here, let me see them." They were decent Hitachi blades, procured who knows where and abused considerably. He ran a fingertip along an edge, felt its ragged burr, and practically shivered with dismay and excitement.

Going to his supply closet, he removed his stone from its oil bath and carried it to the unused counter before his father's chair. He reexamined the edge—a couple of bad nicks to work out first. The other man watching annoyed him, but after a few strokes, Giuliu was lost in it. He heard again his father's voice, felt his father's talc-dry hand around his own, gently correcting, entrusting him even with the delicate texturing shears. A subtle, maddening art, but the old man had never felt a moment, or a blade, wasted in giving his son such a skill. The Hitachis sung as he ran them against the stone, and Giuliu felt himself sliding into the sun-dappled past, back when everything was still good and clear and—

"It is a patient process," Baba said. "Perhaps I should come back tomorrow."

"No, no." Giuliu lurched back to this world. "Here, see it now." He took up a tissue. It wilted away from the blades.

"Incredible! What, please, do I offer you for such a service?"

Giuliu stiffened his jaw. "Niente," he said gruffly.

The other man bowed slightly. "You have my gratitude."

"Repay it by not cutting my boys' hair."

The other man smiled mysteriously, either arrogant or dignified, and Giuliu saw that he wouldn't yield so easily. Baba wrapped his shears in the cloth and, with another slight bow, turned to go. Giuliu looked at the two empty chairs, at his oil-spotted hands. Baba reached for the door, the bells rang out, and Giuliu knew that whichever decision he made, he would regret it.

"Aspetta, un momento," he said. "I have to know. How do you do it?"

One day a week, Giuliu proposed, no more.

On a Tuesday, Baba stood with a towel draped over an arm as Giuliu took his time with Signore Cappadoro, a retired lawyer, who, thank God, insisted on a cleanup every three weeks. That afternoon, the only other visitor was the postman, who brought more bills and stared at Baba like he was a living exhibit. For his part, Baba kept quiet and busy, sweeping up, inspecting the tools and supplies, and learning the levers and positions of the chair. Hesitantly, Giuliu had moved over to the first station, his father's, and given Baba his own. Still, he trembled with exasperation when the man experimentally lathered the ivory-handled, badger-hair brush with which Giuliu had been taught to shave, himself and others. He barely knew what to say to this foreigner and was irritated he couldn't read the *Giornale* in peace. There'd been more drownings in the Mediterranean, news so common he usually recalled only the numbers—thirteen, twenty-four, sixty-three—and cursed the fools for taking such a journey in the first place. Now, with Baba nearby, Giuliu felt odd and put out and skipped those stories altogether.

By the third Tuesday, no surprise, word had gotten around. The proprietor of the café came over and peered in the window. The postman rushed in and out with even greater alarm. Then, just after lunch, a boy Giuliu hadn't seen in months shuffled in, sporting a sweep-over that had grown shaggy and frizzy. He looked at Giuliu guiltily. "Take a seat." Giuliu gestured at the second chair. "I know who you're here to see. Baba," he said resignedly, "get him a cape."

Giuliu felt wounded, wronged—here he was *giving* his job away—but he also found himself fascinated. Baba held the shears as strangely as he did his clippers and made quick, angular cuts Giuliu never would've considered. He was almost disappointed when, in the middle of this display, one of his regulars came in. He gave him a more meticulous cut than usual.

"What is this?" the old guy said when Baba stepped out for a cigarette.

"Charity work," Giuliu said quickly. "Barale put me up to it."

"Ah," the regular said, at a loss. "Welcome the stranger, eh?"

"Shirt off my own back," Giuliu muttered.

Baba took another boy just before close, then, per their arrangement, Giuliu paid him half of what he'd earned, the rest going to chair rental and supplies. This was, more or less, what Giuliu had hoped for, to lure back his old customers, with a little extra on top.

He was unprepared, however, for the following Tuesday. When he came down to open up, seven or eight Africans were lingering on the piazza. After Baba arrived, they came in and sat tentatively in the folding chairs along the wall. Giuliu thought about booting them out, but they looked so hangdog. "Listen," he told Baba, "no discounts. They pay the full amount." That afternoon, Baba saw six more customers, three of them migrants. A local boy came in, a younger teen. He'd made some clumsy attempts, obviously self-done, at side etches, apparently never having worked up the courage to visit Barale's camp. The boy waited nervously next to the Africans, about to bolt at any moment, until Giuliu said, "Come on then, Luca." He started the same cut he'd given the boy since he was five. Then Giuliu paused, stole a glance at Baba, got out his clippers, and cleaned up the boy's zigzags. "Better?" Luca practically beamed at him.

At the end of the day, it was the best take in months. But Giuliu thought of little Luca sitting next to those strange-smelling newcomers, and he knew that this too would already be village gossip. Regret, Giuliu was reminded, was a many-layered thing.

He sat on the piazza with his grappa. The old couples passed by, the mothers, their children. The café grousers sat grousing. Marco was late, and Giuliu had been attempting a little public banter. "Dusty today, isn't it?" he called out to the Raveggi twins, the only single girls in the village. "We'll have another blood rain before we know it!" But they wrinkled their brows at him and hurried on. "Signore Cappadoro!" he called out to the lawyer. "Comandante, your cut is growing out nicely." Cappadoro only grunted and joined his compatriots in the café.

Giuliu was aware of his standing in Erice: a wounded duck, an orphan still chumming around with his only friend. Now and then, Marco dragged him down to Trapani, where they hung around the tourist bars and Marco got hollering drunk with sozzled women off the cruises, occasionally leading one off to a nearby pensione. Giuliu was usually left to small-talk her sunburned friend or apologize to the bartender. He wasn't sure how exactly he'd come to be known as the diffident grump and Marco the rough-hewn, charming lad. He saw his friend crossing the square, stopping to chat with the chubby Raveggi girls—to think the eldest had once been interested in him, Giuliu—who were suddenly all atwitter. And here Giuliu was, flailing in his attempts to mollify his fellow villagers. He couldn't wait for Marco's arrival.

Yet he was terrified of what Marco might say: that Barale had gotten to him too, whispered his cheap pieties in Giuliu's ear. And all of this bullshit about trying to save his business? He was only ruining everyone else's—these stranieri would drive off every last tourist. They'd only suck us dry and move on. Same with Barale, just another miracle worker down here angling for a cardinalship. Well, fuck Rome! Marco would raise two fingers toward the north. Fuck Berlin, and Brussels too! And Giuliu knew he'd immediately agree. Dry-mouthed, heart pounding, he'd be glad for the rough clarity. Don't fret, Giu, Marco would reassure him. Things will pick up. It'll get better. We just have to have to remember who we are.

He saw Marco turn to come his way, and he reached for the grappa and poured them both a drink, ready to feel Marco's burly arm around him, ready to hear him break out into song: Ah, che bel vivere, che bel piacere per un barbiere di qualità!

But Marco veered off into the café, where one of the old farts stood him a drink. He threw only a quick wave in Giuliu's direction, the look on his face so cold and impassive that Giuliu's heart flapped miserably against his ribcage. He sat there, burning with embarrassment, as if the whole village could see his cheeks flush red, then quickly swallowed both grappas and rushed home to his little apartment above the shop.

He needed to do something, to explain to Baba why it couldn't go on. The man was polite enough, he'd take the news without offense—then go back to cutting hair at the old convent and decimating Giuliu's trade. But, no, he had to fire him. For the good of the village.

The following Tuesday, however, Giuliu came out to the piazza to find at least fifteen new customers waiting. Baba stood among them, looking so eager to begin that Giuliu's resolve fizzled. Once again, a busy day began.

In between cuts, Giuliu's couldn't help studying Baba's peculiar methods. The man spent minutes just staring at a customer's head, then launched into a flurry of cuts, from all directions, in no apparent order. He was clearly self-taught, and kept adjusting the chair, spinning it this way and that. Go easy, Giuliu wanted to say, that's an heirloom. "Keep it turned toward you," he counseled instead. "Use the mirror to get a better look." He made suggestions too about the way Baba held his shears and clippers. He'd felt the ache in the wrist that came from poor technique, that could end a career, but, more than that, his pride needed bolstering. He found himself taking care with his work, not just repeating the same cuts again and again. Watching Baba, his fades had already improved. He had occasion too to study hair he'd never before had between his fingers: Africans and Arabs, but also Afghans, Iraqis, Eritreans with their bushy curls. And he wasn't just taking Baba's overflow. Some of these foreigners, the ones with more conservative styles, preferred to wait for him, Giuliu.

Without quite meaning to, he'd upped Baba to three days a week.

"Where are they all coming from?" Giuliu asked him. "They can't all be living at the convent."

"Some come from Trapani."

"All this way?"

Baba grinned. "Yes, they like to look good. And they hear we are two very fine barbers."

Just as likely, Giuliu thought, they weren't welcomed in Trapani's barber shops. In an entrepreneurial spirit, he put out a plate of candied orange and kept a pot of tea steeping through the day. On the radio, Baba played African music, and his customers sometimes got up and danced while their friends laughed and clapped, their boisterousness spilling out into the piazza, where the codgers in the café sat glaring. But Giuliu felt a curious excitement. Many of these new customers actually spoke serviceable Italian, and he found they answered even the stalest joke about Roma FC or the Cinque Stelle with generous laughter. Sometimes he had the creeping feeling it might be at his expense. The swirl of languages—Pashto, Urdu, Bambara, Wolof, Tigrinya—could be bewildering. Still, the extra business had already helped him pay off a few bills. And, in certain ways, it felt more like his father's shop than it had in decades.

He saw, however, fewer and fewer of his old regulars. He'd tried to spread word that Wednesdays and Fridays were business as usual, but on those days he had a nearly empty shop. Passing the café, he could hear the eternal chorus—*That Giuliu, there was always something off*—idle complaint being Erice's real stock-in-trade. The codgers were all unkempt. Wispy flyaways, overgrown eyebrows, thickets of nostril hair—Giuliu itched to prune it all back right there on the piazza. Apparently, they would all let themselves go completely, even the ones vaguely sympathetic to migrants, rather than patronize his shop.

Then there were the boys. At first, he noticed only two or three, boys either he or Baba had recently cut. Their heads had been buzzed to the scalp, uneven, at-home jobs done, no doubt, by their mothers. Some of the older boys—the ones pushing twenty, who didn't have the brains or the guts to go off to university or to work in Palermo or Catania and just skulked around all day, looking surly and lost—had even shaved their heads completely. When Giuliu met them in the pasticceria or the market, he felt so menaced that he hastened his step.

He was aware too of the lingering figure of Vaccaro, the village's sole cop. Usually, he spent his days drowsing in a stuffy office above the bakery. Now he always seemed to be stalking the piazza, taking notes in a little book. Vaccaro had even started wearing his revolver, the barely used leather harness creaking across his belly like an ox in the traces.

Once Giuliu ran into Signora Azzaro. "And how was young Paolo's confirmation?" he inquired solicitously. *Come on, help me out!* he wanted to say. *Your boy is the one who started this mess. Tell me what to do!* "He's a fine young gent," he went on. "He'd make a fine priest, actually." But the woman just stomped off, leaving him with a look to curl his own hair.

He had to content himself, then, with the laughter and cheer of his new customers. None of them really knew him, and he wasn't about to pry into their lives. Midafternoon, Giuliu tuned the radio to the news—more drownings at sea—and the room would fall silent. Sometimes, in the mirror, he'd catch them staring off into space, with expressions of such isolation and longing he had to quickly look back down at his work. "A lot of these boys," Baba said to him one day as they were sweeping up, "they know someone who died coming here."

Giuliu murmured vague agreement. Like Marco said, the crossing was so dangerous only a fool would try it. Well, the foolish or the desperate, Giuliu supposed. Didn't he himself still sometimes dream of Milano, of his mother, of a new life? He could see a hollow watchfulness in their customers' eyes. Eager as they might be for work or money, they were constantly borrowing someone's phone to look at photographs of family back home. It took courage to break away, to roam thousands of lonely miles from everyone you knew and loved.

"You must excuse me," Baba went on. "I am very distracted today."

Giuliu knew these apologies, these prefaces. His father had never been a talkative man, yet he'd said the right things as he listened to the customers in his chair. As a boy, Giuliu had seen grown men, pillars of Erice, confide and confess and even weep, especially when the grappa came out. Men used to come to the barber for bloodletting, to have teeth pulled, for all sorts of ailments. Even now, his father had instructed, cutting hair is not the only service we provide.

Giuliu hesitated, then gestured to Baba to have a seat. He brewed another pot of tea, levered back his own chair. They sat staring at the ceiling. Finally, Baba began to speak.

"I apologize again, sir. Today was a very difficult day."

"You don't have to call me 'sir.'"

"Yes, sorry, Mr. Giuliu. I was just thinking today about my wife and my boys."

"You're married?" Giuliu was surprised. "You don't wear a ring."

"I am afraid it was among many things I sold on the way here."

And then Baba was talking about Liberia, the days when everyone was fleeing the civil war. He and his family left their house in Monrovia and traveled to a town near the border. They were arranging travel documents when the rebels arrived. Everyone knew they wanted recruits and were pulling children into the war. Baba and his wife had told their boys to run and hide, but they were too proud, too protective. Tell them to come with us, the soldiers demanded. They grabbed Baba, held his hand flat on a table. Tell them! One of the soldiers smashed the butt of his rifle into Baba's hand, breaking his fingers. Tell them now! Finally, the rebel commander came in, asked what was happening, and promptly shot his wife and both of his boys in the head. Come on, he said to the soldiers, forget this loyalist swine. They left Baba sobbing on the floor. Eventually, he snuck across the border, through Guinea, Mali, Algeria, and Tunisia, where he paid the last of his money to get on a smuggler's boat, and finally here to Sicily.

Giuliu stayed silent. At this point, his father had usually just murmured something comforting, or poured another round of grappa. But this was not about a jilted mistress or a truculent teenager; Baba had strayed into territory his father had never known. Giuliu thought to ask if the broken fingers were the reason Baba held his shears so strangely. But that seemed a trivial question. The moment came when he should have said something, then it passed.

"Maybe I should not have resisted," Baba went on. "Maybe my boys, my wife, they would still . . ." Now Baba was at a loss. "This job, it is very important to me, sir."

"Giuliu," he said, and faltered at what else to add.

That night and the night following, Giuliu slept terribly. He laid in bed turning over Baba's story. Was the man telling the truth? More than that, how long could this arrangement last? Was he, Giuliu, ruining the promise of all those rich tourists off the cruise liners, Erice's chance at rebirth? He finally dropped off—and was woken by a crash. He ran downstairs and out the front door. In the distance, he heard heavy footsteps, voices, laughter—deep or boyish it was hard to say—and turned to see his candy-striped pole smashed to pieces.

He spent the next few days cutting in a daze, hardly able to meet Baba's eyes, even in the mirror. Baba's day off arrived, and the shop was customerless. Giuliu had been staring at the *Giornale* for hours, understanding nothing, pacing up and down stairs in his head.

The bells rang out. "Well, here I am finally," Barale said as he came through the door. "A little later than expected. Busy as always." He tugged on a forelock of his now almost shoulder-length hair. "We always say be Christlike, but I'm not sure Rome would approve." He laughed, loosened his collar, and made for the chair. "I leave myself in your capable hands."

Giuliu only grunted and stood with his arms crossed over his chest.

"You've taken down your pole. It was damaged?"

The priest damn well knew. The whole village did.

"Must have been the wind."

"My own efforts haven't always been popular," Barale said. "Take heart. We're far from the only ones eager to help. Italy is changing. All of Europe is."

"Change doesn't come this far up the mountain."

"The trick, I've found, is to really get involved in the life of a place. Reach people on their own terms, slowly, a little at a—"

"Sorry?" Giuliu said heatedly. "Excuse me? Do you have any idea what I gave up for this town? To keep this shop open? I could've gone to Milano."

"But why? Was anyone asking you to? Erice would've found another barber."

"Yes, but—" How could he explain? This man looked like he'd never had to face a consequence in his life. "You don't understand this place. You just don't."

"Once you've made a decision, don't let it be your burden. Make something of it."

"Some of us have to live for *this* world, padre."

Barale, at least, would come out of this mess unscathed, gleaming even. The people of Erice would never hold him to account. The priest spoke to their better selves, the ones who would always welcome the stranger, shelter the homeless, feed the starving, and visit the dead, the ones who would ascend, flawless, to heaven. But a barber could only tend to their vanity, the person they had to confront in the mirror each morning. And try as he might to tame their cowlicks, to shape their beards, to hide their weak, quivering chins, to disguise their bald spots, their moles and scars, they kept coming back, ever more ragged, sagging, and wrinkling, decaying under his very fingers.

"You've met this challenge bravely," Barale said. "Not everyone would take such a risk." He paused. "To be in any way . . . different, in a place like this, well, that already takes a lot of—"

"I'm sorry, father," Giuliu said abruptly, "I don't think I can fit you in today." But it was too late. He hadn't been able to control his panicked expression. Barale had seen. Mother of Christ, were they *all* able to see him?

"Papa Francesco," Barale rushed on, "has brought in a lot of progressive thought and . . ."

Giuliu was already headed upstairs. "A shame, father," he called back, "you had to come all the way up the mountain."

The following Monday, Baba came in limping, with a black eye and a welt on his forehead. "Minchia! What happened?" But Giuliu had already guessed—the boys, no doubt the same ones who'd broken his sign—had known from the beginning that something like this would occur.

"Ah, it is nothing, Mr. Giuliu. Simply an injury from playing football." Baba smiled. A crackle of pain lit his eyes. "Some of my friends, they can get quite competitive."

Baba, he wanted to say, you can tell me the truth. But he also knew Baba wouldn't identify anyone or risk a stir. His only choice, like all stranieri, was to lie low and hope things blew over. Another long day began. Giuliu felt his guts churn every time he saw his fellow barber grit his teeth to get through another hour on his feet, another cut, those Hitachi shears not making it any easier. The mood in the shop was subdued, everyone staring at their phones, no one mentioning Baba's black eye.

Baba wanted to stay and help sweep up. Giuliu sent him home to the convent, and couldn't even bring himself to take up the broom. He wandered out into the streets, searching in his fellow villagers' eyes for those who knew what had happened, for an answer, and only finding himself back in the piazza, where a few harried tourists were shielding themselves from a stiff, gritty breeze. A crimson sun floated on the scratchy, copper-tinged horizon, the sirocco turning everything hazy and unreal, the breath of the Sahara curtaining the sky, catching in his nose and throat. All over Erice, doors and shutters were closing, people sealing themselves up inside.

The next day, it was blowing even harder. Giuliu sat upstairs, sipping then gulping grappa while grit skittered against the windows. At midday, the sky opened up, rain stoning down, the cobbles and gutters running red. Giuliu felt himself trembling, about to explode. Finally, he couldn't take it. Pulling on his shoes, forgetting his coat, he reeled out into the storm.

Marco opened the door. He stood in his boxers, two days unshaven but his eyes bright as blades. "Minchia, it's three in the morning. What are you doing pounding like that?"

Giuliu stumbled into the apartment. There were football magazines stacked on the coffee table and *Montalbano* playing on TV, the music sawing ominously under a lingering shot of police inspecting a flinty Ragusa beach.

"This fucking storm," Marco said roughly, going over to the small checkered sofa and dropping heavily onto it. "At least I don't have to read another goddamn meter this week."

Giuliu swayed in the middle of the room. "Marco, I . . . I need your . . . to talk to you." In a blur, he explained: His pole getting smashed, Baba beaten up, no way of proving which of the boys had done it. If he accused any of them, all of Erice would turn against him. But if he said nothing, it would only get worse. Baba was the first—what about all of their customers? He just wanted it all to stop. He just wanted to cut hair and—

"Oh, shut up," Marco said. "I smashed your sign. And Vaccaro and I beat up your man."

"What?"

"Giu, I'm trying to save you from yourself. When was this ridiculousness supposed to end anyway? Apparently, neither you nor Babbu got the message."

"But you—" Giuliu started. Then, as the truth crashed down on him, he raced on about Baba, about Liberia, the soldiers, Baba's wife and sons. "Everything he's been through!" Giuliu knew he was in the right now, and felt the power of this coursing through him. "Don't you understand? Baba came here to be safe, so that something like that never happens again!"

Marco picked at something on the sofa, looking weary and unimpressed. "And I suppose you believe everything they print in the *Giornale* as well?"

"No, Baba isn't like that. His fingers. You don't know him. He's—"

"He's after a job. *Your* job."

"We're . . . we're *friends*."

"And he knows your school? What grades you got? He remembers your dad?"

Giuliu felt his knees giving way. He dropped down beside Marco on the couch. Instead of socking him in the shoulder, Marco put his arm around him. Giuliu realized he was sobbing. "I don't know," he said. "I don't know what to do."

"It's okay, amico mio," Marco said. "Don't worry. We'll take care of it."

He felt Marco's arm warm and tight around him. A stream seemed to be rushing inside of him, pushing him helplessly forward. He turned and kissed Marco, half missing his lips, feeling his stubble rough and oily against his own cheek.

"Minchia!" Marco shouted.

"I just thought—" Giuliu began. "I just thought you—"

Marco shoved him away. Giuliu sprawled to the floor. Marco knelt above him, eyes burning, fist cocked. "Go," he said through gritted teeth. "Go before I do something."

Giuliu stumbled down the stairs and out into the sizzling rain. He lurched back to the shop, clambered up the stairs, aimed himself at the closet. There he kept a shrine, photos of his father, the one photo he had of his mother, half of her face turned away, so that he had never quite seen her. In the center of all of these relics, the holiest of all, wrapped in lambswool: his father's shears. German steel, sharpened so many times the manufacturer's stamp had worn off. The shears Giuliu had learned with—he'd never known how perfectly balanced until after his father's death, when he'd put them away and bought his own, inferior pair. He held one blade and pushed up his cuff, exposing his wrist. "This is how you test them," his father had said, shaving off the fine downy hairs. Giuliu started to do the same, angling the blade more and more steeply, the blue veins under the pale skin starting to stand up. Just one, he thought. One cut would be enough. A fat, dark drop of blood welled up . . .

The air burned bright and hot. He woke on the floor, smelled the tinge of iron and the vomit all down his shirt. He'd thrown up before he'd passed out. From the piazza below, he heard the old men in the café, eternally babbling. He thought he heard knocking downstairs, but it went away. All he could do was drag himself down to the shop to retrieve another bottle of grappa. As he was digging among the supplies, the knocking returned. He cursed under his breath, tasting bile again.

It was Baba. He let the man in, in order to tell him to go away, go away forever.

"Mr. Giuliu!" Baba said. "Are you all right?"

Giuliu looked down at his shirt, at the dried blood on his arm, then straggled over to the wall of mirrors. A stringy-haired old man stared back at him. Without thinking, he took up his shears and started snipping.

"But what are you doing?!" Baba exclaimed.

"I've been cutting it myself for years."

"No, no, it won't do." Baba reached for a cape and flourished it over his chair. "Sit now."

Giuliu made a brief show of protest, but if he stayed vertical another moment, he'd vomit again. He sat stiffly as Baba parted and re-parted, considering from all angles, squeezing a few spritzes from the water bottle, to see the contours more clearly, just as Giuliu had taught him.

Then Baba started in. From the roots up, Giuliu felt himself bristling. He heard the shears singing in his ears, felt the slight, not unpleasant tug of the blades. Baba brought out the clippers, and their familiar whine brightened his headache, made him squint and wince. Baba took down his sideburns, faded his sides, going tighter and higher than Giuliu would have done himself, less cautious in the spots where Giuliu could see, but not quite admit, that he was thinning and graying. The middle of the cut, where the customer saw only his lopsided, unfinished self in the mirror, was the chasm. Now he felt his own self-loathing, all of the years he'd wasted, right there before him, naked and raw under the unrelenting shop lights.

But as Baba took off the frazzled split ends and made them lay down, as he worked lines that Giuliu himself wouldn't have guessed, something else was taking shape. He thought of the evenings when the old man would put him in the chair and instruct while he cut. Baba brought out the straight razor. The hot foam on the back of his neck, the gentle bite of the blade—Giuliu shivered. With a scalding towel straight from the warmer, Baba wiped the foam away with quick, hard strokes. Then he molded another towel over Giuliu's scalp and started rubbing with skull-thrumming vigor. Giuliu felt every capillary opening, every follicle letting in heat and oxygen and a strange pulsing energy. Then Baba dropped the chair back and gave him a hot shave—smooth, fast, assured, just as Giuliu had taught. And his father before him.

Lastly, there was the fuzz around Giuliu's ears, his wayward eyebrows, the stiff, coarse sprouts from his nostrils, with which Baba was no less meticulous. Giuliu couldn't help drifting away, back to those years of tutelage, when he dreamed of taking everything his father had shown him and going off to Milano to ply his trade. Like his mother, he'd always longed to see more than could be glimpsed from this mountain. But then, too soon, the old man died. And Giuliu couldn't stand to let go—all of the salty jokes and unguarded, grappa tears, all of the years of smoke and talc—couldn't stand to see the shop close and leave Erice hollow at its core. He couldn't break that promise. So he had to fire Baba, tell him to leave, go far away. And if Baba refused, Giuliu would call the Ministry of Health. Such were the conditions at the convent that they might shut the whole place down. When his fellow villagers saw what he'd done, they'd accept him again. They'd take him back in. They had to.

His father had told him there would always be work, for a barber of quality, always. But what use was a middle-aged Sicilian—no matter how many cuts he knew—in a city like Milano? Even if, up there, they'd barely notice one who was different.

"Okay," Baba said, "so I think now we are finished."

But Giuliu didn't even see the face in the mirror that looked so clean, so unburdened. He was too deep in the past, remembering what his father always used to say at the end, as his son gazed at his reflection with a gathering sense of possibility and the chance, always, for change: *Ah, now, who is this strange boy?*

"Aspetta," Giuliu said. "Un momento."

He went upstairs and found his father's shears where he'd dropped them in the sink, washed off the blood, and carefully wiped them down. Then, testing the blades, hearing them schnik perfectly against each other, he took them back down to the shop.

"Please," he said, placing them in Baba's mangled hand. "Please."

THE SUBMERGED

When I was fourteen, I lost my virginity to David Flower, the future congressman.

My parents had moved us, the summer before, from Cambridge to West Virginia. They were junior co-hires in public health at WVU, but they wanted to live way out in the country, in a hamlet named Glory, to be closer to their research: tainted groundwater and its correlation with cancer rates, stillbirths, and other misery. Of course, Glory was also, as the locals said, real pretty.

That fall, I started at Glory Unified High. There he was in homeroom. "Welcome, Dave," the teacher said, and David Flower corrected him. The other boys wore camo jackets, lewd novelty T-shirts, their crimson and gold football jerseys. David had only khakis and an Oxford, tucked tightly in. Sometimes he came in the uniform of the Royal Rangers, a Christian scouting organization. By the end of that October, we were going steady. Lonely finds lonely.

The next several months were all hand-holding, kissing with the barest flicker of tongue, and David risking quick touches of my breasts or butt like he was going for a cactus. I never went to Glory Baptist with him, though I did twice see the inside of his house. The first time, his mom was passed out on the couch. The second, I witnessed his dad hurl a softball trophy at her. I asked my parents if we should call the cops. My dad frowned and said, Well, there was more to an education than AP scores.

After David got his learner's, we drove to the Monongahela River in his father's pickup, which had a crunched front bumper from a crash with a parked car. Beneath a black willow, in a spot selected for its beauty and seclusion, David laid a blanket out. "It's okay," he said, "because I know we'll always be together." After, I found that I hadn't bled. I felt flush all over, like when I sat close to a campfire. In a husky voice, David told me he loved me. Then he got up, ran to the river, and, with a whoop, launched himself into the water.

I didn't have to break up with David. I just made new friends. While he stayed after school to study or attended prayer meetings, I shot off in smoke-filled cars to smoke-filled parties. Junior year, I got my septum pierced, and he received a medal for his Ranger achievements.

One humid April evening, I was sitting on my porch watching lightning bugs. David Flower came out of the muggy dark with his ash-blond bangs plastered to his forehead. "Hey," he said in a strangled voice, "I was just walking by." For an odd, stray moment, I was sure he was going to ask me to marry him. But he only wanted to talk to my parents, about Yale, where they'd done their PhDs. He'd been accepted to WVU. Or he could go into the armed forces, see what the GI Bill would pay for after. My dad, who wouldn't even watch war movies, told David to go into the navy—better food, less chance of getting killed—and that, in five years, he'd write him a letter of recommendation. My parents always liked David Flower. Or maybe they were amused by him.

A friend threw a graduation party, and I was surprised to see David there, wearing a faded orange polo and drinking a beer, wincing with every sip. "I can hardly believe it now," I told him, in reference to our year of dating. "Crazy!" he answered, wincing again. There, in the basement of my friend's house, David and I had sex for the second time. I'd been with six boys and one girl since him, but I played with his hair and thought fondly of that afternoon by the Monongahela. "Did you get a merit badge for losing it?" I teased him. "Or did they take one away?"

Twelve years later, I was living in New York, running a fledgling green architecture firm with two guys I knew from Columbia. I'd been engaged to their best friend, a Marxist architectural futurist. After three years, I'd moved out, took the first "jr 1BR prtl Hudson vu" I saw. My partners stopped socializing with me, but I wouldn't abandon the firm. Commons Collective had a mission. I wanted to be on the crest of the wave.

We'd recently put up a website. That was how David found my address. "Remember me?!" read the entirety of his initial email. An odd blip in a hectic day. The year after I graduated, my parents had left WVU for Stanford. Everything about Glory felt hazy now, like a dream or a period of illness. I was scrambling to put together a competition entry but dashed off a reply: "Of course! Where are you now? Hope yr well."

David wrote right back, at length. He'd gone to Annapolis—never made it to Yale—and now served on a Los Angeles–class submarine at the rank of lieutenant commander. He'd been all over the world. Or all under it! His message was all exclamation points and question marks. "I believe you must be doing very well! in New York City!?!" It turned out he was married—they'd met at church—with two boys. Twins! He'd just taken them to their first Royal Rangers Camporama!

Where was all of this going? I wondered, scrolling to the bottom.

"Hey, Liv!" No one had called me that in years. "Ever see the inside of a sub?!"

Two months later, I rented a car and drove up to New London, Connecticut. As I pulled into the base's visitor lot, a man climbed out of an old pickup. He was fit and tanned, taller than I remembered. His ash-blond hair was buzzed to the scalp. I gave him a quick hug.

"Meat pie?" David reached into the truck and offered me a pastry in waxed paper. "Great Greek diner down the road. I was stationed on Crete a while back."

"Sorry, vegan."

He shook his head, chuckled. "You always were setting the trends!"

He nibbled the meat pie and said, "It's great seeing you, Liv. Funny saying your name, hearing your voice, after all these darn years. Nothing whips you harder than time, right? Yes, ma'am, I believe that's right!"

"Let's go see the sub," I said.

David locked up the truck. Same model as his father's, I commented. "This *is* Dad's truck! Brought it up from Glory after the old man croaked from lung cancer, restored it part by part—gotta love a vintage vehicle!" I thought that an early nineties Ford wasn't exactly vintage but said only, "Sorry about your dad."

At the entrance to the base, a sign read, "Submarine Capital of the World." It was in the shape of a submarine. A couple of security guys patted me down with an air of intense gravity, as if holding their sphincters tightly.

We walked up a long drive flanked by rosebushes, cannons, white bungalows, and ugly warehouses. Then the docks came into view, the Thames River inlet a deep, flat indigo. There were two submarines, grim and sleek with mottled dark gray and black panels. David led us to the sub on the farthest dock. After we crossed a gangway, a hatch swung up, and the top half of a sailor appeared, wearing a Navy cap and blue digital camouflage. "Ma'am, welcome to the U.S.S. *San Juan*." I wondered why, under the sea, down in the dark, encased in a thick steel tube, it was necessary to wear camouflage. But I just said, "Thank you," and accepted a hand down.

The cap, ducking through the bulkheads, hustled us along a tight corridor and into the command room. He barked out, "Civilian onboard!" Four other sailors pulled black fabric scrims over the screens they'd been scrutinizing. In the fluorescent light, they were moon-faced, pubescent—thin mustaches and steel-frame glasses. "Ma'am," they said in turn. "Ma'am." "Ma'am." "Welcome, Ma'am."

"At ease," David Flower said, though they already appeared to be.

"Lieutenant," they said. "Lieutenant." "Lieutenant." "Lieutenant."

David pointed out the piloting station, the sonar station, fire control, the NAV Star, the Type 2 periscope, the Type 18 periscope . . . As men often do, he was trying to charm and bewilder me with expertise. But the cap kept hustling us along. The crew mess: steel picnic tables, faux-wood paneling. The galley: every surface scrubbed to an operating-theater shine. The crew bunks: tiny and meticulously made.

"Jesus," I said, "you sleep in these how long?"

David sent a little twinkle toward the cap, but the other man just stood with his arms behind his back. David barely had time to comment on the engines, the twin carbon dioxide scrubbers—"Mary-Kate and Ashley"—or the huge, cauldron-shaped nuclear reactor. In the torpedo room, the torpedoes were painted an oddly merry green.

We passed into a chamber where eight pairs of wide, tall cylinders stretched from the floor through the ceiling. "Tridents! The *real* peacekeepers. For ending the world, or making sure it stays in line! Go ahead," David Flower said. "You can touch one."

He gave me his shy smile again, then swung back and slapped a missile hard. "Safe as Sunday school!" A low, hollow roar rung up through my feet. I hesitated, reached out.

Thirty minutes later, I was straddling David Flower while he thrust awkwardly inside me. We were in the passenger seat of the truck, parked in a lonely clearing near the Thames. I wriggled him deeper inside me; he came with a gasp. I hurried up and got there too. We extricated ourselves. I stepped out onto the grassy bank, rearranging my bra and black tee. "That was unexpected," David said, buckling up as he joined me.

"Oh? So you got in touch, invited me up here, just to try the meat pie?"

"And you came to see the sub?" he said, grimacing. Under his khaki shorts, he was already coming back up to half-mast.

"Looks like the *San Juan* is readying to fire again."

This kind of talk wasn't me, but I couldn't help making David squirm, for old time's sake. He laced up his bright white running shoes, tried to put his arm around me. I shrugged him off. "It's okay. You don't have to ask me to the school dance now."

David hacked out a laugh. "Liv," he said, "you're the only one I know like you."

For a few fugitive moments, I was back on that bend of the Monongahela, its sluggish current glinting under the lacy black willows. I remembered that I'd worn a royal blue bikini under a red sundress, that we'd swum for hours, the water warm and silty, David's ash-blond hair shining in the hazy sun.

On the drive back, he told me about his marriage. The months at sea had taken their toll. He and Bonnie Rae had prayed and prayed, but they were just looking out for the kids now. (I could see him scanning the floorboards, in case he'd left a bit of condom wrapper down there.) He was coming ashore, going on reserve duty, maybe starting up a defense contractor consultancy. Citizens didn't comprehend how much was being done, in secret, in their names. Americans were uncomfortable that we were conquerors—Hollywood, Wall Street, Apple computers—that our military, the "Silent Service" in particular, was the only thing truly holding *Pax Americana* together. As we pulled into the base, I wondered if this speech, rather than the quick screw, was the reason David had asked me to visit.

"There's folks," he said, "been submerged. Running silent. But they're rising. You'll see them rising." I heard that familiar, strangled voice, so certain, so searching.

"Hey"—I let out a jangly laugh—"our physics teacher, what was his name?"

"Who, Mr. Rendell?"

"Mr. Rendell! Remember he shot that baking soda rocket through the ceiling?"

"And he used to wear his adult Space Camp uniform to school!"

We sat there in David's father's pickup, laughing, swapping memories I hadn't even realized I'd forgotten. "It is morally reprehensible to romanticize the past," my ex used to say. But, well, it'd been a shitty year, and maybe it wasn't just a quick screw that had brought me here either.

Lieutenant Commander David Flower's first campaign email was poorly designed. A posed photo of David, Bonnie Rae, and the twins. Red, white, and blue letters spelling out "Family values and dedicated service you can trust." Blocks of text on his humble upbringing in "coal country," his love of our great nation, love of the Lord, and Naval commendations, all capped by a paean to staying the course overseas, and underseas.

It'd been eight months. I'd guessed he'd felt too guilty to be in touch. Apparently, he hadn't gone on reserve just to spend more time with the boys. And the consultancy was on ice too. "Somehow, I'm not surprised," I wrote him. "Congrats and, despite my better principles, good luck."

I hesitated, then added that I'd be in Connecticut again, to do a quote on an "eco-lux" B&B. Not exactly the People + Planet > Profit ethos Commons Collective sought to chart, but it'd pay the overheads for another month. Geoff and Stefan, my partners, said I had a knack for client outreach. More likely, their pride wouldn't let them grovel for the job. A week later, David emailed back, reluctantly it seemed, to suggest we meet for lunch.

Instead, we checked into a motel. "Rush hour on I-95," David said, half-panicked, as I undid his belt. "I need to be away by four."

"Oh, please." I pushed him, hard, and he fell back on the bed. I tugged his khakis down and got on top. "How's fundraising?" I said between sharp breaths.

"Phone calls," David huffed. "Phone calls, phone calls."

"They ponying up?"

"They're all with Whidbey. The incumbent. His family owns. An island."

I rolled off and told him to suck my clit. He went about it more accurately than expected. He made love like a troop of scouts fixing a busted dam: earnestly and with rising alarm. "Maybe go back to Glory, run from there," I said. "Local boy makes good."

"Right. They'll bring out." He was laboring away. "The fatted calf."

The few men I'd dated since my ex had all been sleek and hairless, obsessed with whittling their bodies with esoteric powders. David had solidity, beefiness. He looked up at me, fished a pubic curl from his mouth. "Is there anyone in your life, Liv?"

Three years spent trying to share, not to mention decipher, my ex's vision for "new modalities of co-dwelling in the post-Anthropocene floodscape"—it'd been thrilling, and exhausting. Architecture: in which every man fancies himself an engineer of the soul and treats every woman, even his fiancée, like an intern.

"Does it matter? You're just here because you're bored of blondie back home."

"Bonnie Rae is a woman of God. But she's also a good mother."

Women like her—practically an advertisement for some Christian dating website—hovered like a photo negative over almost every interaction I had with men. Still, why the hell did I find myself annoyed with *her?*

"I didn't come to talk about your family. Tell me you want to fuck me already."

"Oh, I really want you, baby," he said with singsong irony.

I rolled my eyes, grabbed him again. "Say you'll fuck me so hard I'll scream."

"You're going to be screaming in a second."

"Make it a little longer than that. And say 'fuck,' goddamn you."

"I'll fuck you so long"—he gritted his teeth—"I'll fuck your fucking eyes out."

I sputtered with laughter, now completely inflamed. There was still something virginal about David Flower, and I didn't know whether I wanted to preserve or defile it.

"I'll fuck you so hard they'll call the cops."

"All right," I said, "get to it then."

Lieutenant Commander David Flower lost his primary by twenty points. In an email to his supporters, he lamented that the Silent Service—so essential to our great nation's security, but ultrasensitive—was hard to make a calling card. We needed to acknowledge the sacrifices of our servicemen and women, the months and years at sea. Also, he'd failed to make inroads with Whidbey's bloc of middle-aged Catholic professionals.

David emailed me personally to say that the country was broken, nothing made sense anymore, no one ever thought about everything being done behind the scenes, they just kept on spending and spending, enjoying the spoils without owning up to the conquests, maybe it *would* take another 9/11, or worse, to make them realize the real realities. I thought of my ex, who'd ranted longest whenever he had a paper rejected. You almost felt sorry for men. The older they got, the more their principled outrage and thwarted ambition grew indistinguishable.

Over that year, David and I met nine more times, at different motels and hotels. When I introduced anal and toys and several other things I considered pedestrian, David Flower's eyes shone like he was dangling his mortal soul over the flame. After, we'd talk about Glory. The switchback gravel roads, the bleached-out shacks, the hills thick with pitch pine and scarlet oak, all buzzing with insect life, the Milky Way spilled across the dark night—David could make it all come swimming back. Sure, there'd been the mines, the stringy burnouts who'd share their dope then spew hate, David's parents screaming so loudly that you heard them half a mile away. But . . . that river running warm and silty and slow, the lacy shadows of the willows, David's hair glowing in the sun.

Once, after another breathless session, he rolled over and let out a sigh like an air mattress collapsing. I thought he was about to rue his decision, or non-decision, to stick it out with Bonnie Rae. They'd gone to counseling, with a minister. "You got past the first sin," I said. "Don't tally up all the rest."

"I was thinking on all those college kids."

Another unimaginable massacre already receding into the daily horror. "Well, if your people didn't let everyone carry a fucking artillery."

"How could God let that happen?" David's eyes burned with hurt and ardor.

"Come on," I said. "Don't ruin the mood."

"He spoke to me once."

"Oh, fuck me . . ."

"I was thirteen. I hadn't even met you. At Camporama '86, He came right out of the fire, sat down beside me, told me to help working folks all over the country. Help put food on their tables and protect their homes and to always, always keep families together."

"As he goes truly messianic," I said, "my last bit of horniness drains away."

"If I was there, I could've done something."

"Right, arm the professors so we can have a real bloodbath."

David took my hand, squeezed it. "Hey, how are your folks?"

"Tenured," I said. "Zero worries. Not packing heat, yet."

"We keep asking Mom to come live with us. But, honestly, I—"

"You're allowed to hate them. You don't owe your fucking parents a goddamn thing." But I was talking to a man still driving his dad's pickup.

David reached up, touched my face. "You know where I come from, Liv. There's no one else who does. Maybe that's why I feel the way I do."

He kissed me on the lips, pulled back, held me with those burning eyes. And then, goddamn him, he told me he loved me.

That year, I found myself in countless meetings, massaging planning commissions and placating floppy-haired CEOs, two of whom wanted to meet in their homes, in case I might fuck them or give free decorating advice. Still, Commons Collective was finally breaking even. It helped that everything was exploding. Whenever I went up to Connecticut, the few remaining mills and sagging saltboxes were like rotten teeth in a big money smile.

But I'd been sleeping terribly. I was back in the *San Juan*, down in the groaning dark, rivets popping out of bulkheads, David's face buried in the periscope, water hammering in, columns of smoke and fire pluming from the Hudson, Tridents roaring into the night, searing phosphor white—the sun flashed across my prtl vu of the river, and I woke with a start, my heart thunking all around my chest. "Commander-in-Chief's got his finger on the button," David said once. "We're what's on the other end."

One afternoon, I took a lunch with the head of a philanthropic foundation, a woman in her late fifties with the taut, shiny skin of a dolphin. We chatted about their flagship project, solar-pumped latrines in sub-Saharan Africa, and ordered off a menu that would've paid for a hundred of them. Halfway through my pitch for their new headquarters, the Dolphin paused in her langostino risotto, said, "Oh, don't fret. You had it when you walked in." Yes! I shouted to myself. Yes! This gig would make us. Geoff and Stefan could suck it! Then the woman laid a waxy hand on my wrist. "Olivia, you're such a good face for your firm." When I stepped outside, I felt like I'd been slapped. Twenty years in the trade, and I was still just a token.

David and I met two days later, at a Quality Inn overlooking I-95 that made me feel cheap and lonely. He slid in, not fully hard, and I nearly said forget it, forget all of this.

Instead, I told him, "Say, 'You're such a good face.'"

"You've got a great face, Liv. A beautiful face."

"No, 'You are such a good face.'"

"Really," he said, "you're beautiful. I want to fuck your—"

"No, not that. And don't call me *Liv*."

"But I never used to—"

"Say, 'We don't care who you are. What the fuck you think. We just care about your face and your smile, your tits and ass, and not even another *woman* will take you seriously.' Fuck! You're thinking it, so just say it! Jesus, you'll say anything to get laid!"

David's forehead beaded sweat, plastering down his hair. "Liv, I don't know what you're . . . I love you. I loved you the moment I saw you."

"Oh, fuck," I said, "just shut up." Then I sobbed and rambled: "You think you'll be fine, you're doing the right, necessary thing by leaving, then you wake up three years later, half the people you loved *still* aren't speaking to you, and all the green-fair-upcycled-shared-sustainable everything you killed yourself for is now just empty slang batted around every boardroom in the country." I wanted to disappear, I told David. I just wanted gone.

He held me until I ran out of breath, murmured in my ear: I was brilliant, I worked so hard, deserved to be rewarded, deserved everything. We lay in each other's arms between those ultra-bleached sheets, and, wrung out, I fell asleep—next to the Thames, the Monongahela, the Hudson, the water flat indigo, muddy brown silt, a sheet of burning white light—and then David was standing over me, buttoning up his khakis. "Rush hour, got to scoot. Liv, I love you, I love you." And I heard myself, a thousand feet below the surface, saying it back.

Solar toilets and the Dolphin got us through the crash, barely. We'd grown to twenty—I'd even had my own intern—and now we were three again, doing our own renders, frantically bidding on every executive suite and Westchester remodel in sight. A decade ago, I'd have toasted the market melting down. (I'm sure my ex popped a bottle of Prosecco.) Now I just felt my career staggering down an alley to lie down and die.

That February, a flier arrived at my work, glossy card at once slick and crude: "Lieutenant Commander David Flower, Fire Back for *Your* House of Representatives" on a black background with other words seen through a periscope's sights—*Taxes! Wall Street! Socialism! Evictions!*—all about to be blown to bits. The nautical, or subnautical, theme continued for weeks. Once Stefan plucked a flier from our inbox like it was a soiled napkin, then saw my name on the label. "Flirting with the enemy?"

"Mailing lists," I mumbled, "you know . . ."

I should've asked David to stop the fliers, but I almost admired his doggedness. Plus Stefan's and Geoff's heads exploded every time another came in. On the flipsides of the fliers there was always some rant about the dark forces assailing the American dream, but I was too exhausted to read them. Our man had been in the White House less than six months, and already the bloated old men were calling for "insurrection."

Since coming ashore, David had gotten doughy around the middle; the way he settled into the mattress, and I settled into him, felt oddly comfortable. He was always on the road, campaigning, eating crap, falling behind, despite his assault on Francis Huntington Whidbey—now referred to by his full name—a Wall Street errand boy, meeting in private with the president, in the pocket of every bank he'd bailed out.

"You're anti-spending? You were in the goddamn military."

"I just say what they tell me," David murmured into the pillow.

"What who tells you?"

"I had to remortgage the house. I'm signing the boys' future away if I don't win. No way you can't take their money."

I wouldn't let him play victim. "Christ, you'll be putting Obama in your crosshairs next."

"That tested well. But we didn't want any calls from the Secret Service. They want me to change my name. Flower is 'too soft' for a soldier."

"Change it to what? Colonel Kilgore? Major Disaster?"

For a moment, I thought I'd hurt him. Then he cracked a smile. "Dick Armey."

I half laughed at that.

"Actually," David said, "I've met Dick. I like him."

David's platform, idiotic as it was—how could Obama be thick with Larry Summers *and* a Socialist?—was everywhere. David's new handlers might be hideous mutants, but they weren't dumb. No way our man would get reelected, if he didn't get shot first, just too many homes and dreams gone underwater. But, in the end, I was afraid to protest harder, afraid, despite my better principles, of losing David. He was still insisting we meet at different hotels each time. Bonnie Rae had a PI on his tail, he said, to prove him guilty, so she could exit the marriage untarnished, a good, Christian divorce.

I'd crawl out of bed to shower while David brushed his teeth. We'd stand before the misted mirror, and I'd see myself in her place, run ragged by the twins, packed lunches, permission slips, oil changes . . . But, then, I was thirty-eight. What did I have to show for it? An apartment I'd never own, a career that kept me verging on a breakdown, a chunk of cultural capital that impressed others but no longer meant much of anything to me.

That fall, I saw David on cable news. The pundits were saying that his virulent TV spots had taken their toll on Whidbey. Footage of one of David's rallies showed him thumping a podium—"Connecticut, *you* built it, *they* took it!"—as a roomful of white folks nodded and clenched their jaws. Once I was down near Wall Street for a meeting and wandered through Zuccotti Park, to see the Occupy camp. It smelled of wet socks and curry. On a makeshift stage, various impassioned people in rain gear were delivering speeches. The whole time, some homeless guy was cavorting in front of them, dancing and leering. The constipated-looking citizens at David's rallies would've had him hauled out in a heartbeat.

It seemed David was making headway; he actually had a chance of winning. But when Whidbey prevailed, the news only made wry puns—no one really cared about a regional primary, only the larger "insurgency"—Lieutenant Commander David Flower, torpedoed and sunk. And there was a photo of him I hadn't seen before. He was smiling so desperately, he looked like he was being choked by his own necktie.

The sex mellowed, grew tangential. Sometimes we'd just lie in bed, and I'd play with David's hair, which, though thinning, had somehow stayed blond. I bitched about work, and David rued his debts. He'd be lucky if he kept the house, if the boys could go off to college, if they had a change of church clothes that year. "My whole life I've been losing," he'd say. "My whole life they've been mocking me. But He took the scourging, endured it for us all." David sighed at the motel ceiling. "Give me strength to endure."

I felt worn to threads too. My fortieth was marked by a party with Geoff, Stefan, and various clients, including the Dolphin. My social circle had broadened, or slumped, to include people who defended stop-and-frisk and thought the cops had been right to turn their backs on the mayor. I only murmured vague agreement; we got most of our work from these ghouls.

A week after my birthday, David gave me his graduation yearbook. I'd thrown mine out years ago. There I was, awkward and miserable in Docs, hair bleached and fried the same as all the friends I'd never spoken to since. More than ever, I felt time as a stream, swifter each passing day. How long had I been swimming against it? Maybe now I was content to let it carry me backward, if only I could grasp a few lost things.

I was still sleeping horribly, my dreams of atomic fire routine yet terrifying. I fantasized about leaving the city, dropping my practice, going right to seed. Each time we concluded, David dropped me at the Metro North, scrupulous to arrive just before the train and never linger. As my train, all the trains, all the honking and buzzing cars and trucks funneled into the city, I remembered the method my mom had taught me to catch flies, a cone of paper poked into a bottle of vinegar, and all the flies just clamoring to get as far down that bottle as they could.

One night in the Village, on my way to a dinner, I passed the New School, where some event was kicking off, a crowd gathering. I was pushing my way through, colossally annoyed, when I heard a voice. "Hardly recognized you."

I was in the kind of clothes I wore to meet our clients, Balenciaga on my shoulder. My ex was in his old black hoodie, fingerless gloves, and what appeared to be a sarong.

"Here for the lecture?" he went on when I could summon no words.

"No, why? Who's speaking? You?"

My ex scoffed. "We're here for the demonstration." He mentioned the name of some idiot far-right "provocateur."

"That guy? Why waste the energy?"

I waited for his usual speech. Instead, he just said, "Geoff and Stefan were right."

"And you're still adjuncting, I'm told."

He broke into a grin with one front tooth missing. I recoiled. "A little scrap at the last one of these," he said proudly.

Besides the tooth, he looked good. I felt sudden remorse, the vertigo of standing atop a mountain of decisions, large and small, from which it seemed impossible to climb down.

"Taking any punches tonight?" I said.

"Only one way to find out."

I was about to ask how long the protest would go—just the kind of question he'd always criticized me for—in case there was time for a catch-up, a couple of drinks . . . but someone started up with a bullhorn—*No platform for hate! No platform for hate!*—and my ex turned to bark it back. Four years together, we'd been here so many times that my throat tickled with a gathering shout. Then, coming out of my daze, I remembered my dinner, for which I quite literally couldn't afford to be late, and I rushed away.

When I saw David next, I was hectic. He immediately started talking about home. But now, instead of bright slivers of memory, it was slabs of rhetoric. "A place like Glory centers you. Grounds you. People took care of each other. Good people. Good work."

"Your parents tried to kill each other. And your dad got cancer from that mine."

"I'm not talking about then. I'm talking about before then." Then he ranted about coal, China, the unions, elites, Catholic professionals. For a moment, I wished I'd brought toys, a strap-on, but I was too jangled for even that rough catharsis. "The problem with liberals"—David was worked up like he hadn't been in months—"is they care more about people drowning halfway around the world than—"

"Tell me something," I said.

"What?" His eyes flashed like he was ready to talk dirty.

"If I went back, back to Glory, got a teaching job or something, would you come with me? The twins are nearly out of school. Do Bonnie Rae a favor, forget Lieutenant Commander David Flower, just come with me. We'll get a cabin on the Monongahela. We don't have to wait. We can just disappear. We can, we can—"

David took me by the shoulders, locked eyes in a way that made me flinch. "Okay."

"What?"

"I'm in. Everything you just said, I'm in."

He told me to give him six months, to get his consultancy started, get an LLC up and running. The way he spoke, to hear him say he was ready—I was floating. All the way back on the train, I was on that bend of the Monongahela, watching the willows feather the lazy brown current, kicking lazily to stay afloat, watching as the boy I loved finally came to join me.

We met again three weeks later, mid-May. The sex was uneventful. I didn't come, but I didn't care. Time was opening up. I could feel that stream purling through my fingers and toes, as if the motel bed were gently rocking as I showed David property listings on my phone. There was the question of a dock, whether we wanted a little dock, a little boat to tie up. Everything was impossibly cheap down there. It was all shimmering into view.

I almost skipped the shower, to carry David's scent back to the city with me. But I had another dinner, one I'd hardly given a moment's thought to except to dread it. David got in with me. There under the water, I truly didn't care where I needed to be. I closed my eyes, pressed my head against his chest.

Finally, I got out, picked my black jeans off the floor. A new email buzzed on my phone. Usually, I waited to look at my inbox until after David dropped me at the train. But I had a sudden hope it was from my client, canceling or postponing.

As David stepped out of the shower, I stood there, brandishing the message on my screen.

"What?" he said, startled. "They sent that already?"

"Don't 'they' me. What the fuck are *you* doing? How can you say *any* of this?"

Part of it harkened back to the old ads against Francis Huntington Whidbey. Now, however, there was talk of "Fat Francis" allowing illegals to go on crime sprees across the state. There were photos of Whidbey shaking hands with bearded Syrians, cast with a fuzzy gray filter to look like surveillance footage when, on closer inspection, they were taken at a barbecue. "Weak Whidbey," the message read, "terrorists come on in!" Dave Flower, on the other hand, was calling for watch lists, roundups, deportations, raids on noncompliant businesses. "America for Americans!" And the photos: Dave shooting pistols and machine guns, holding up the glassy-eyed head of a deer (I'd never known him to hunt), standing in a military cemetery, wearing dress uniform and a severe expression. Dave and Bonnie Rae posed before a huge cross, she in an idiotically short skirt. And finally, one of Dave pointing what appeared to be a military-grade rifle in the direction of another photo of "Whining Whidbey, Agent of ISIS."

I shouted. I screamed. All this horseshit about refugees and terrorists and "illegals"—what happened to his fucking family values routine? Was that just not selling this year? "You actually *believe* this shit? Or you don't, and that's worse. Are you goddamn . . . hollow?" But what really enraged me—I was furious at myself—was that he'd just ripped Glory from my grasp. It'd never been anything but a desperate dream, but I'd convinced myself even still. "Have you always been completely fucking hollow?"

"Liv, come on . . ." David clutched his towel as if to ward off a blow to his groin. Neither of us could look directly at the other but met gazes in the misted-over mirror. His placid blue eyes and ash-blond hair . . . I brandished my phone again, like a badge, like a totem. "This," I said, "this is everything I've spent my life fighting against." He just kept staring at me in the mirror, with a blankness that left me flailing, an emptiness that only sent my own voice echoing back. "Just because your parents were crazy rednecks, doesn't mean you get to . . ." I sputtered. "You don't get to! You don't get to!"

And, hearing myself, I wondered if what I'd really wanted all those years was the luxury *not* to fight. All those times I could've ended it. All the rooms where I'd crawled into bed with David Flower and somehow never believed it could be true, that any of this was actual life. In that moment, I wanted my rage. But all I had was grief.

"I'll ruin you," I told him, gesturing at myself, my body. "I'll go to the media, tell them the God-and-country candidate has been whoring around, and that she's a fucking Socialist. Card-carrying." At one time anyway. "I'll end you. Bonnie Rae, everything."

But I understood: He hadn't been insisting on all of these different motels in case Bonnie Rae found him out. I'd just made it explicit. He was only worried for his career, for the destiny he'd thought he was owed since he saw God come out of that campfire.

I reeled out of the room, stood on the railing overlooking I-95, jabbing at my phone, trying to summon a car from the ether. I walked around the motel twice in the haze now turning to rain. I could've gone to reception, asked for a cab. Instead, I went back to the room.

David stood in his khakis and a U.S.S. *San Juan* T-shirt but with no socks on. His hair was still wet, his face waxen and slack. He tried to embrace me. He asked me to stay, we'd talk it all through, he'd go home that very night, confess everything to Bonnie Rae. I couldn't speak. How had I been so foolish, so sure he'd go with me? Next to his devotion to that destiny, I didn't even qualify as the other woman.

"They think I can win," David Flower told me in his strangled voice, tears streaming. "I need you, Liv. I love you. I always have. I don't know who I am without you."

I let him drive me to the station, but we were late, a train just pulling away. I sat there, watching the rain needling the hood of David's father's truck. We were both quiet, stunned. I closed my eyes and saw the Thames, its dark, flat indigo stretching out. I saw the Monongahela, sluggish under the lacy shadows, two children on its banks with nothing between them but a sundress and a faded pair of swim trunks. I saw my Hudson, and I was back in my dream, far below the surface, lights flickering, the whole vessel groaning. I kept screaming at David, but he had his face in the periscope. Water sloshed around our knees, our hips. He emerged from whatever he'd targeted, shouted something about the escape hatch. But the floors and steel walls were shuddering. It was too late. We were trapped. We were going down together.

IN THE LEAVES

They found the fifth body a mile and a half into Schnitke's woods, and then, after combing another mile, Hansen found the shooter. The rifle lay in the leaves beside the shooter's body, from a distance just a lump of dark green parka, threadbare corduroy trousers, and work boots. He was lying face up, showing what remained of his left cheek. He'd flinched, Hansen guessed, or tried to pull the rifle away at the last moment. But the second shot had done the job. Hansen called out for the other men from the rescue squad and police, then tore his eyes away from the wound.

It was cold, even for late November, the ground hard with frost, the air so crystalline Hansen could hear every crackle of the police chief's radio—*Shooter down, repeat, shooter down*—as the others approached through the trees. They all stood looking at the ripped-apart face, the expressions of the other men almost deliberately blank, not wanting to betray anger or fear or revulsion, rookie stuff. Most of the rescue squad were part-timers, and among them, Hansen was unremarkable: skinny, pigeon-chested, with deep-set, lusterless brown eyes. He usually wore a mustache but had recently shaved it off, leaving a patch of skin above his lip that stung in the cold wind.

Dispatch had said there were five men in the hunting party, five victims. The first they'd found was Old Schnitke—beard, sunglasses, a dribble of chew down his chin—shot in the legs, stomach, and chest. Then his grown son, Carl, twenty feet from his father, blood stains spreading all across the back of his camo coat. The other three bodies were likely relations; Old Schnitke never let anyone but family hunt on his land. Hansen was a hunter himself and knew that these four hundred acres, all hills and good ground cover, were laced with deer trails. Wherever there was a high vantage, Schnitke had put up a stand. Hansen turned and looked up at the nearest oak. Sure enough, a blind thirty feet up, chunks of two-by-four nailed into the trunk for steps.

A burst of static on the chief's radio startled him. He tried not to show it.

"Jesus, he just opened up, didn't he?" the chief said. "Just rained down on them."

Hansen found himself staring at the shooter again, the long, rubber-dark hair splayed out on the brittle leaves. "You know who that is, right?" he said.

"Sure do," the chief answered.

"You surprised?"

"Nope. Is anyone?"

It was four-thirty, the sun already going down. Hansen was standing at the open window, sweating in an Admirals T-shirt, when he heard Luce clumping up the stairs. He went to the stove, stirred a cup of instant, sat heavily at the kitchen table.

When she came in, he immediately saw how pale she was. She leaned in the doorframe, prying off her boots, said, "You could've come to my place last night." She kept her heavy coat on, went to the sink, started putting away his dishes. "God, how can you stand this temperature?"

The last week and a half, the thermostat had been broken, so it kept the radiators working all day. Hansen had them all closed off but one, and even that was enough to roast. He'd been keeping the windows wide open, and every few minutes a breeze billowed the curtains into the room, then sucked them flat against the wall again.

"Too exhausted to go anywhere but here," he said.

Luce came to the table with her arms held tightly across her chest, bent over, kissed him quick on the lips. A strand of her red-brown hair blew over her face. So pale, he thought, she looked like she'd been boiled in salt.

"Who was it?" she said. "They haven't been saying on TV." She sat down, flicked through a coffee-stained issue of *Outdoor Wisconsin* on the table, as if that might have the answer. "It was Joe Bee Cheng, wasn't it? They'll put him away forever."

Hansen shook his head. "Shot himself."

Luce blanched and, for a moment, sat staring into Hansen's nearly bare living area. With her high forehead and gently concave cheeks, she often seemed beautiful to him. Sometimes she was the image of her Norwegian mother, who'd made the crossing alone back in the late sixties, pregnant and with little English. New York, then Milwaukee, then here.

"Some people just aren't built right. Should've locked him up years back."

"Chief never had enough to bring in him," Hansen said. "Wife wouldn't press charges."

He thought to explain further, but Luce reached into her purse, brought out her pill tray, started lining them up on the table: light brown caps, dark red gels, white tabs the size of dimes. *Alpha Lipoic, Lecithin, Mito-6 DNA Repair* . . . Her goddamn "longevity" pills.

She went to the sink for a glass of water. When her back was turned, Hansen swept the pills off the table and into his hand, then took up the tray as well. Without turning to him, Luce said, "You toss those, I'm out sixty bucks."

"Then I give you thirty. You know the deal." He went to the open window. "Why didn't I dump your ass when I found out about this shit?"

He squeezed the pills in his fist until the sticky outer coatings started to come off, then dropped them out of the window, down to the mud, melting snow, and engine and lawnmower parts that was his backyard. He dumped out the rest of the pill tray as well and tossed it back on the table, wiping both hands on his jeans.

"Fucking asshole," Luce said.

He didn't reply, just went back to his coffee. After a few minutes, Luce began pacing. "Let's go somewhere," she said. "How can you stand this temperature?"

"Mixed Emotions?"

"Jesus. Fine."

Hansen got his wallet and keys. As they were crossing the gravel drive to his junked-up Plymouth, Luce stopped suddenly. "Hey, wait," she said. "Give me that thirty first."

"Don't trust me?"

"No, sir. Not no one."

On the way to the bar, Hansen thought about what had been on the news. On TV that morning, he'd seen aerial footage, the state police in the woods, doing their crime-scene work. There were interviews with folks from Sawyer County: Old Schnitke's ex-wife, Joe Bee Cheng's nearest neighbor, a woman claiming to know Joe Bee who Hansen didn't even recognize. Footage of hunters walking the streets of Hayward and pickup trucks with bucks tied to the beds. A shot of the Hayward fishing museum: a huge fiberglass structure shaped like a northern pike. It must have looked ridiculous, Hansen thought, to the outside world.

Then there was background about Joe Bee. Hansen knew most of it. A couple of decades ago, the government had started settling Hmong refugees in Saint Paul and Minneapolis. Most of those left the Cities for little towns in Minnesota and northwest Wisconsin—more like how they'd lived back home. Joe Bee's father had fought the Communists back there in Laos, and that had led, eventually, to visas for the younger Cheng and his family. To a tumbledown, vinyl-sided house on the outskirts of Hayward, little ones running all over the place. The TV said the Chengs had kept to themselves. It also had a couple of items Hansen didn't know: Joe Bee's real name, Alang Bee, and that he'd been in the National Guard for a year, had gotten sharpshooter training. Well, if Hayward folks knew one thing about the Hmong, it was that they were hunters and liked guns. Hansen saw the bumper stickers every now and then: *Save a deer, shoot a Hmong.*

He'd been out to the Cheng residence once, with the squad on a domestic. Cheng's wife had been messed up, her cheek split open, a busted chair lying in the corner. She'd "slipped," wouldn't say different. But the whole town knew about those scenes at the Pick 'n Save, Joe Bee cussing her out in the middle of the cereal aisle, the little ones clinging to her like they were still in a refugee camp or something. A couple of years back, one of the papers out of the Cities had run some human-interest features on the Hmong, photos of them dancing in traditional dress, embroidered tunics, big silver jewelry. The Cities crowd loved that kind of stuff. But Hansen had seen the trashed inside of that house, the wide-eyed kids peeping out from the bedroom. They never put that in the human interest.

Luce tuned in the local station as they drove into town. They had the story too, plus speculation about what had set off the shootings, if racial language had been exchanged, who shot first. One announcer was making Schnitke out to be some beloved member of the community. Schnitke was just a blowhard with four hundred acres and a snowmobile rental business to his name. Hansen had been through it with him. He did small-engine work on top of the rescue squad, had fixed Schnitke's rentals for a time, until he figured out that the old guy never paid. No one deserved what had happened to that hunting party. But the way Hansen saw it, maybe Schnitke had asked for what he got just a little too hard.

At Mixed Emotions, he and Luce sat in the corner. Hansen ordered a fried walleye basket and an old-fashioned. Luce just had an iced water, part of her fasting routine. She had a couple of days off from her job running craps at the Sevenwinds. They talked about what they'd do, maybe drive down to Eau Claire. Or, if the weather warmed up, go to Mill Bluff, hike around all those weird white sandstone buttes that jutted up out of nowhere. Luce said she could use the exercise. It was brisk walking, not running, now. Better for the joints, she said, because those had to last a long time.

Four bearded men in hunting camo came in and sat at the horseshoe-shaped bar, draping their heavy coats over their stools. Maureen, the bartender, lined them up four Point Specials.

"You fellas giving the deer a little break?" Maureen said.

One of the men had a tattoo creeping up his neck. He was bald, red-faced, had already been drinking. "Shit, we'd be swimming in deer guts if all that bullshit hadn't scared them off," the guy said. "Give us Buds, not this pisswater. And a round of that brandy back there."

Maureen was a big, broad-shouldered woman, had stared down a lot of hard customers. "This is the closest we got to Bud." She started popping the tops on the Point Specials. "Hell of a thing what happened. Let's get the edge off."

The other three men murmured their agreement. But the guy with the tattoo wasn't dropping it. "Maybe this'll teach those squirrel-eaters to start respecting private property. Dude was lucky it wasn't my land."

"Fucker," Luce said under her breath. Hansen just went back to his lunch. The guy was drunk, didn't know what he was saying.

But Hansen found that his ears were still pricked up, listening to the four hunters getting rowdy, breaking one another's balls about all the deer they hadn't bagged, throwing around tough talk about how they'd act under live fire. A burst of laughter went up from the bar. They were joking around like it was just another day.

Hansen heard himself, as if from a distance, clearing his throat and saying, "Some folks are trying to eat here. This ain't some militia clubhouse."

The tattooed guy slouched himself off his bar stool, came over to their table, stood smirking down at them. "Who are you, friend?"

I found the goddamn body! Hansen wanted to shout. Instead, he said, "I never seen you around. We lost some neighbors today. Get your head out of *Soldier of Fortune*."

"Neighbors?" Up close, the guy reeked of booze and deer scent. "What, you some squirrel-eater too? Don't got it in you to stand up for your own people?"

Despite the anger welling in him, Hansen felt deflated. He didn't know Joe Bee Cheng, didn't feel anything toward that family other than sorry for the wife and kids. But Hansen did know that these bearded fucks were everywhere now, and that the guy's smirk told him he was only being baited. He half wanted to take a swing, but he was just too exhausted. And this was Maureen's place. This was the town he'd been born in. No sense in trashing it.

Hansen licked his chapped upper lip, strange without the mustache, ready to say something anyway. But just as he began, Maureen called out, "Hold up now!" She flipped up the hinged section of the bar, came out, and took the bearded guy by the arm, almost courtly, and led him back to his stool, casting a reproachful glance at Hansen. "All right," she said, "four shots of brandy. They're on me. Courvoisier. Best I got." There it was, Maureen needed the business.

The four men started drinking and laughing again, casting mocking looks at Hansen all the while. Hansen made a sign for the check, but Maureen waved him off. Next time. Before there was more trouble, he and Luce slipped out.

"Good," Luce said. "We don't need that kind of stress. Takes months off."

"Piece of shit," Hansen muttered at himself, balling up his fists.

The next day, they just went out driving, as far as a half tank of gas would get them and back. They went up along Lac Courte Oreilles, where they saw men out in flat-bottomed boats fishing for muskie, even as ice was already skinning over the lake. They drove out into the countryside, past squat ranch homes and cabins with deer strung up in the yards, through fields of late-growing soy and chewed-up stalks of corn, and then came back hugging the Namekagon River, stopping for fifteen minutes to kick around the old dam and the millpond and the ruins of the timber sheds that were all that remained of the big mill that had once been the heart and blood of Hayward. Finally, they turned back toward town.

Luce's apartment was half of a prefab duplex on the north side. Her windows looked out on the skeleton of the next building in the line of the development. It'd been sitting unfinished for over a year. Inside, Luce's place still felt new, even with all the family photos and the old tasseled quilts she had hung and all the big, leafy plants overgrowing their pots. It was cozy enough. But then there were all of the emptied cardboard packages in the garbage. *VidaPure, Cell Defense, Reversatrol.* At one time Luce had kept her army of pill bottles lined up on the kitchen counter. Now Hansen could hardly talk to her if they weren't hidden out of sight.

They were just supposed to be killing an hour before going to play euchre with a woman Luce knew from the casino and the woman's brother. But Hansen felt a sudden, unbidden swell of desire, took Luce by the hand, drew her into the bedroom, down to the mattress. He kicked out of his jeans, pulled hers off, came back up her body, pressed his lips against the hollow of her neck, slipped his fingers into her underwear . . . But Luce pushed herself up and away. She rocked back onto her knees at the end of the bed. The humiliation at the bar, he must have thought about it loud enough, because Luce said, "Nothing you did. Just don't have the energy right now. Hell, I got to change up the mix again. Nothing feels right."

Hansen rolled onto his back and closed his eyes. Six months after he and Luce had started dating, the rescue squad got called out to her mother's house. He'd been there in the back of the ambulance when the woman passed. A stroke. Gone quietly. Even if we'd gotten to her in time, he told Luce. And he'd been the one to do it too.

That was what it was all really about, Luce's supplements, filling up with so much of the fucking stuff she was poisoning herself. Her mom had been fifty-nine, too young. The first time he'd confronted Luce about how much she was taking—she'd dose herself four times a day when she had the cash—she'd just smiled, said, "But what if they're right?" Oh, yes, her "research," the obscure magazines and glitzy websites, all of their hidden causes and miracle cures. It can just happen, he wanted to tell her. Sometimes your number just gets called. But it all came from her grief, and he knew better than to barge in on that. And, hell, maybe her mom's death was the very thing keeping them together. Two years now. *Don't go*, he sometimes whispered when he lay awake next to her sleeping body. Well, he had his own crazy fears.

For a moment, all he seemed to see were the ends of his eyelashes. Then his eyes refocused on the bedside clock. They'd both fallen asleep. He nudged Luce awake.

"Euchre?"

She moaned. "Too late now. I'll call and apologize." She arched her back, stretched like a cat, rolled over, lay her head on his chest. "Know what I like about you?"

"You were calling me an asshole and all that the other morning."

"The quiet. You're so quiet."

"I talk. I'm talking to you. Told that prick at the bar to go fuck himself."

"Stress, too much stress." Luce made a gentle tutting sound. "But I still like you."

Somewhere in the far distance, there came the dull knocking of a woodpecker. For a moment, Hansen slipped back into dozing, then woke himself deliberately. "Like me? Or love me?" He nudged her. "Hey. Did you hear?"

She undid a button of his shirt, curled one of his chest hairs around her finger. "What, you need reassuring all of sudden?"

"You not wanting to fuck me don't help."

"I told you already, need to get my pep up." Luce's expression clouded. "You think Schnitke said something to set him off?"

"Don't want to hear about Schnitke or Joe Bee neither."

"They're from another culture. He was probably hunting to eat."

"Don't even know where I'm goddamn living anymore."

"Yeah, well, we're all trying to get somewhere."

Hansen turned her off his chest. "Give me that thirty bucks back. Your shit is making us both broke."

She scowled, rolled over again, away from him. Why couldn't he take her by the shoulders, shake it all out of her? But it was too deep. It would never budge. He started to say something, but she was already asleep. *Luce,* he whispered after a time. *Please, don't.*

Midafternoon the next day, he went down to the fire and rescue complex to ask if he could punch in for a few hours. No small-engine work this time of year, especially now Schnitke was gone. But Hansen looked so bleary, the squad captain just sent him home. He lay on his sofa in his underwear and socks, clinging to his comforter as the sun flashed its last light against the window he'd left open to the cold.

The news footage played again in his mind. All of those aerial shots, floating up above it all, just another five-minute tragedy. Cheng had put six bullets in Schnitke, plugged one of the others right in the base of his neck. Even with the rifle Cheng had been carrying—a cheap semi-auto, just a catalog gun—he'd wiped them right out, clean and quick. The Hmong had fought a war those dipshits at the bar could only fantasize about. A war that'd been dirty as hell. Some people aren't built right, that's what Luce had said. But it would've taken a lot more than hard words to make a man snap like that. A lifetime of shit would do it. Maybe from birth, their fault or not, some just get aimed straight at death.

Hansen rose, paced his apartment, moving through the layers of heat and cold, throwing curses out into the dark shapes around him. Easier to have someone warm lying beside you, terrifying when they were gone. When Luce woke in the morning, there was always bewilderment in her eyes, as if she were surprised to still be herself, the same bed, same man, same photos on the wall. But Hansen had to get away. There was work in the Cities. A guy he'd gone to high school with managed a cold storage warehouse over there. Within the week, he could be on a shift picking frozen food orders. What, after all, was even left here?

He flopped back down on the sofa. The temperature soared, plummeted. Just above sleep, he found himself in those woods. His feet stirred the leaves, but the trees above him, the scrub ranging out to the horizon—nothing else moved. It came to him with little more than a change in the light, the graying of the sky: He wanted to find Cheng again—half his face torn off, that sick flesh flower that bloomed when the bullet went in—to imprint that image again, though it was all he saw every time he closed his eyes.

He startled awake, thought he heard Luce clumping up the back steps. It was just a branch knocking against the building. The sun was pushing itself over the horizon. He pulled on long underwear, jeans, his heavy coat, ready for the cold, for what he needed to do.

Thirty minutes later, he pulled to the edge of a gravel track overlooking a shallow valley crowded with black walnuts and bur oaks. In spring, green coming back on the trees, he wouldn't have been able to pick out the small clearing in which the blue vinyl-sided house sat, but now he could see right down into the backyard. A clothesline pegged with children's trousers swinging stiffly in the breeze. A leaf blower in pieces on top of a graying picnic table. A heavy nylon rope strung between two tree trunks, for hanging and dressing deer. Hansen cut the lights and the engine, and when it got cold in the car, he sat on his hands, watching the wind shuffling leaves across the yard. Finally, a light went on, the kitchen, and a figure came to the window and began to work at the sink.

The hair was shoulder length, but from a distance, Hansen couldn't see if it was the wife or one of the daughters. What age would the oldest be now? Twelve, thirteen? In town, Cheng's kids walked with their heads down, always averting their eyes. He'd never gotten a good look at any of them. The figure at the window worked steadily, dipping away every few minutes to gather more dishes. For a moment, Hansen felt a connection dance out between them—that they were both awake and aware at such an hour—then he shut that thought off and got out of the car.

He gently opened the trunk and brought out the soft leather case, slipped his rifle out, running his half-numb fingers over the cold steel and smooth-grained stock. When he turned, the figure at the window had disappeared. A minute later, she came back. He took up the rifle, adjusted the scope, sighted her. Cheng's wife. She wore a man's flannel shirt. It hung like a sail from her tiny frame, her thick, black hair draped over its worn shiny shoulders. As she worked, she stared out the window, off into the distance, her face drawn, exhausted.

She was as opaque as any stranger, yet he'd knelt over her husband's body. He might even have been the one to bring the news: She was suddenly free of his wildness and violence. But did she feel released? Now she and her kids were alone, in a place that might never feel like home, thousands of miles from the one they'd left. Was she grieving for Joe Bee, wearing his shirt, despite everything? How could she even be doing this simple task, the dishes, without falling to pieces? Her face wavered in the crosshairs, his hands trembling. His finger twitched toward the trigger. He drew a breath, steadied himself.

Just then, her expression perked up. She'd seen something. He swung the rifle to follow her line of sight. Then he took his eye from the scope, didn't need it to see the ten-pointer, a trophy buck, picking its way across the yard. It rubbed against the picnic table, marking it, went under the nylon line, and back into the trees. He raised the scope again, to watch Cheng's wife watching the buck disappear. She smiled, the briefest acknowledgment of the fleeting creature, then her face went slack again. Hansen couldn't help shivering. His quick, heavy breath plumed in the air above him. Then he lowered the rifle and was himself only staring off into the distance.

At Luce's apartment, he scratched his key into the lock, went in, and found the pills behind a row of photo albums in her bookcase, where she thought she hid them from him. He pulled the albums out, hazily flipped through one—snaps of Luce's mother, sepia-toned portraits of the generations back in Norway—then dug out the pill bottles. Fourteen of them. He gathered them up, went into the bathroom, stood over the toilet, ready to flush them all. Then Joe Bee's torn, destroyed face floated back into his thoughts. He dropped the pill bottles into a little basket holding spare toilet rolls, turned to the sink, and rubbed water into his eyes until he felt the sting of his early waking subside.

He went into Luce's room, stood watching over her. In sleep, she was never anxious or frantic, never fighting what couldn't be beaten. He took off his jacket, folded it neatly, ceremoniously, on a chair beside the bed. He did the same with his shirt and jeans. And then he lay down, down in the leaves, and closed his eyes beside her.

THE HUMAN CONDITIONAL

I arrive at the refugee center rattled from my bike ride through Piazza Venezia, hungover from too much prosecco last night. I brace myself, then go down into the church crypt. It's late June: Crossings are back up, lots of new guests. Maybe seventy guys are lined up for breakfast—rice and egg (low cost, high protein)—and for the resources room—donated clothes, shoes, backpacks, Bic razors, tiny bars of hotel soap.

I see a few familiar faces, fist-bump with the Africans, shake hands and put my hand over my heart with the Middle Easterners. It's loud, hectic, a little smelly. But there's Danielle, helping a couple of guys with their asylum paperwork. And Rob's teaching the alphabet to a grateful cluster of Eritreans. Jessie's showing a group of study abroad kids around, educating them about the plight of refugees in Italy and beyond. Romans call this place "la chiesa Americana." We're all expats—I've come to write a novel, take a year off from the shit show back home—but few of us are here to worship. We just want to help, do our part to beat back the tide of indifference and hate. Already I feel my headache lifting, my sour stomach settling, my mood blooming and brightening and—

"My friend, my friend, come stai? How you today?"

"Ahmed," I say without enthusiasm, "ciao."

He limps toward me in his shabby knee-length coat and baggy wool trousers—midsummer, no less—and I gird myself for whatever line he's about to sell.

"My friend, you come for the singers?"

"What?"

"The singers." He gestures in Jessie's direction. "American singers."

"What, these college kids? They're just looking around. Are you coming to class?" I ask flatly, hoping he isn't.

"You think I need learn? My friend, I am translator. For Coalition Forces, United States Marines. But they leave me behind, leave me for dead. Your army, my friend."

"Right, sorry about that." I try not to be brusque. We never judge anyone's story, who does or doesn't deserve our help. But every visitor we get, Ahmed tells them the United States Marines betrayed him, abandoned him to the Taliban, Al-Qaeda, whatever. Then he asks for five hundred Euros. "Shoot," I say, "late for class. See you in there?"

"Yes, yes, I want learn better." Ahmed scratches at his balding head. He's in his mid-forties, a decade older than me. I leave him there, eyeing the study-abroad kids. "Yes, English strong language," he mutters. "Make money all over the world."

If Sarwar comes to class every day, I write on the board, *he* _______ *learn quickly*.

"Okay, the conditional!" I begin. "We remember from last week, sì?"

My students smile and nod back at me. I have about a dozen today, all men as usual. Scanning the room, I recognize half of them but only know three well: Tareq, Mamadou, Sarwar. The others come and go—Germany, France, Belgium, Denmark, Norway—traveling illegally on some rumor of good work or good camps, only to get continuously deported back here, where there are neither. But hope dies hard, and everyone thinks they'll eventually make it all the way: the UK, America.

"We use the conditional to talk about what *might* happen, yes?"

More nods, more smiles. The guys are so eager, and so deferential, that it's hard to say when they understand and when they're utterly at sea.

"If Sarwar comes to class every day," I begin to read aloud, "then he—"

"Will!" Tareq immediately answers. "He *will* learn quickly."

"Okay, Tareq, benissimo!"

Tareq is my best student—he did a masters in hotel management back in Algeria—but I have to restrain him from answering every question before the others can finish reading it. Sarwar squints at the board, gears turning so visibly it's both thrilling and excruciating. Suddenly, the clouds part. He raises his hand, clears his throat, and . . .

"If . . . ?" he says. "What mean 'if?'"

Why am I surprised, yet again, just how far back square one can be?

I labor to explain—how *do* you define "if"?—casting about for the Italian. A real ESL teacher wouldn't let other languages in, but, here, it's mere survival. Even giving the guys enough English to hawk selfie sticks by the Colosseo would be an impossible win. Our work is necessary, vital, urgent, even if, if . . . Shit, what the hell is the word for—?

"Se!" It comes to me finally. "'If' is 'se.'"

"Sì, sì . . ." Comprehension blossoms again on Sarwar's face. "'Se' è 'se'!"

Italian feels like someone just made it all up and left out half the letters. We offer lezioni di italiano here too, but most of the guys don't take them. Admitting they're stuck here, after all, would mean giving up on the dream.

If Mamadou gets his EU allowance, he _______ buy a phone card to call his family. I put out a hand to hold back Tareq, let the others answer this and a few more easy ones: the first conditional, for things that are likely to happen, the present smoothly becoming the future. But, already, I need to engage Mamadou. He's sitting in the back, whispering in French with his Malian buddy. "Mamadou, what do you think?"

"Hein?"

"Bienvenue," I say, smiling, "want to try number five?"

If Mamadou calls his family, they _______ _______ be so afraid for him.

I coach him through the answer. Coming to Europe has been a shock. Sure, it's safer than home—an Islamist insurgency has shredded most of northern Mali—but Mamadou keeps getting bounced from camp to camp and then out on the street. Two months ago, he got roughed up by Lega Nord thugs, came in with bruises all over. They took his money and his phone; he couldn't call home for more than a month. "I think my family have funeral for me," he told me. Ever since, he's struggled to pay attention.

"His family, they, they . . . Ils ne sont pas terrifiés pour moi."

"In English, please."

"They will be . . . Je pense que . . . They will be happy, not so afraid, oui?"

"Okay, right, well . . . Close enough! Moving on. Number six."

If Sarwar studies English every day, he _______ improve enough to make friends. I call on Sarwar, and he slowly—slowly—sounds out each word—"If Sarwar stud-ies En-g-lish ev-ery . . ." until he gets to the blank and draws just that.

"Remember last week?" I say patiently.

". . . then he . . . do . . . im-prov-eh?"

He pronounces it with an Italian inflection. Sarwar came here from Afghanistan six years ago. He was a farm boy—the Taliban murdered his father and older brother for participating in a Coalition-funded agricultural project—and probably didn't have any school past ten. He comes to more classes than anyone, and his English still backfires like a busted motorino.

"Good, good. But what comes in between? What word for future tense?"

Sarwar's expression goes misty.

"Remember," I say, "what's *my* name?"

"Teach-er?"

"No, my name. Il mio nome e . . ."

"Will?" he says speculatively.

"Benissimo! Will is short for William. Now try it in the sentence."

". . . then he w-ill-i-am im-prov-eh . . ."

Okay, well, close enough to close enough.

We move on to the next few, all about work. *If he washes dishes for forty hours, Tareq will _______ sixty Euros.* In the evenings, Tareq toils at a pizzeria out by the airport. They exploit him ruthlessly, but he's one of the few with any work, period. *Tareq will be promoted to waiter if he _______ the menu in English.* An optimistic scenario, but optimism is required here. First conditional, the language of possibility. If clause, main clause. Premise, result. State your dreams clearly enough, they can start to feel all but certain. *If Tareq succeeds as a waiter, he will _______ his own restaurant.*

"Yes, open!" Tareq says. "Very good. I can open restaurant. Big restaurant!"

His eagerness propels us. I keep going, letting them learn the pattern on these easy ones, building confidence. My part-timers are all chiming in. Even Sarwar gets one right. *If Mamadou can afford a lawyer, he will _______ his whole family to Italy.*

"He will . . ." Sarwar begins, "*bring* his famiglia . . . ?"

"Eccelente! Molto, molto bene! Bravissimo, Sarwar!"

He blinks a few times. Then he beams. Tareq and several others actually clap for him. This is going to be one of those days when I come out of class walking on air. I almost want to bow, have Sarwar take one too.

Then the door opens and Ahmed grimaces in.

"Have a seat!" I boom. "We're just getting started!"

He ducks his head in what seems apology and shuffles to the front of the room. As he brushes past me, I get a whiff. Like many of the guys, Ahmed smokes constantly (the Italian government rations them cigarettes), but it's also the exhaust palling the streets and something like campfire smoke clinging to his greasy, sweat-sour coat. I suddenly wish to be away from here, sipping an espresso or a prosecco in some jasmine-decked piazza, getting down to work on my novel, my savagely comic dispatch on middle-class, middle-American, middle-brow anxiety. Ahmed winces into one of the tiny desks—okay, he does want to learn, he's just embarrassed to ask, but I'll take a challenge, I'll always, always give them the benefit of the—and then he pulls out his phone and plugs it into a free outlet. He's just here for a charge.

I won't let him kill our momentum. "Okay, time for the second conditional!" *If Tareq started working as a waiter, he _______ send home money for his daughter's surgery.* Several guys call out "will," still following the earlier pattern.

"Quasi," I say. "Almost. Anyone know the better answer?"

Tareq puzzles it out: "Would . . . ? Sì, sì, I would send money!"

Tareq's eagerness shows all of his stifled ambitions, everyone counting on him back in Algeria. His parents spent everything they had to get him on a boat from Tripoli, all so he could end up . . . here, in this basement. I give him one I know he'll like.

If Tareq _______ la lotteria, he would buy a house for everyone in his family.

"Won! If I won the lottery." Tareq smiles hugely. "Ah, but if I won, I make my own hotel. Not just houses. Hotel. Hotels! Like your president. Strong businessman."

Inside, I sigh. We've got more to teach here than grammar.

I pause to explain the second conditional: for things that are unlikely to happen, that aren't impossible but require either a vigorous application of will or a total shifting of the planets. "You have to try hard. Very, very hard." *If the Malian government, the Tuareg, the Islamists, the French military, the Chadian military, the UN Forces, and ECOWAS negotiated another ceasefire, then Mamadou would go home.*

"Difficile," Mamadou murmurs, "très difficile."

Both the question itself and the likelihood of such a thing ever occurring—okay, I took an extreme example. Time to lighten things up. "Let's talk about football!"

If Messi played against Roma—I write in the answer—*he* would *score many goals*. The guys laugh. Jokes at the expense of Rome's luckless club always land. "Your turn!" *If Roma won the Champions League, everyone ________ be very surprised.*

An Eritrean in the corner gives it a shot. "I think is . . . *will* be very surprise."

"No," I say gently, "we need the past tense of 'will.' What is a tree made of?"

"Sì," Sarwar says confidently, "leaves!"

"Good, good. But what else? A tree gives us . . ."

"Would!" Tareq and Mamadou both call out at the same time. They bust up again.

"Oui, oui," Mamadou says, "c'est vrai. Would be very hard for Roma to won!"

Everyone's laughing. Sometimes the best we can do is just give them a break from their worries. ("What mean 'won'?" Sarwar asks. "Like 'won, two, three'?" Otherwise, everyone's nodding along.) We move back to job stuff, how to get them employed, give them a future. I start to mix in the other conditional verbs. *If Mamadou could get a license here, he would be a mechanic again. If Tareq worked just as hard as the Italian dishwasher, he should be paid the same.* Would, could, should—each a different shade of probability, of obligation. Tricky, but we're getting through it, finding a rhythm, everyone's loving the lesson, I've got them in my palm. Then I hear—

Ding. A moment later: Ding, ding.

Ahmed's phone sounding an alert. He's hunched over his screen, right leg stuck stiffly out. Allegedly, he took a bullet in his calf when he too passed through Tripoli. He says he got caught in a firefight between rebels and Gaddafi loyalists. Probably he just fell off a motorino. I stare at him as he digs at his bald head, exposing a sweat-ringed armpit. I'm doubly irritated to realize I've been performing for him.

Ding. I clear my throat. Nothing. I pause, let some silence enter the room. Ding. I glare down at the next question in my notes. *If Sarwar went to pick olives in Calabria, he could rent a room this winter and wouldn't be homeless.*

Instead I read aloud, deliberately, "If *Ahmed* went to pick olives in Calabria, he could blank some money to rent a room and . . ." He stays hunched over his phone, oblivious. I write the question on the board. I read it *again*. He glances up, grimaces at me.

"What you say?"

"Welcome!" I say, jocular and basso. "You're here already, get involved!"

"Pick olives? Why I pick olives?"

"It's . . . it's just an example."

"Ah!" He points, as if catching me out. "You ask you use my name? You ask my, how you say it . . . my persimmon?"

"This isn't an asylum interview. I'm not . . . Anyway, it's 'permission,' not—"

"Ah, I'm joking! I'm having joke with you. You don't see? Joke, my friend."

Once Ahmed came up to me, head hung low. What's wrong? I asked. My friend, he in the hospital. Oh, I'm sorry, I said, I'm so sorry, thinking his friend, like Mamadou, had been beaten up. Then Ahmed grinned wickedly. Why you sorry? He a doctor!

"Right, very good. Good joke. Very funny. Okay, does anyone know the answer? If Ahmed went to pick olives in Calabria, he could blank some money to . . ."

Tareq starts to answer, but Ahmed cuts him off. "No, never. Me, pick olives? No, I am translator, my friend." He waves dismissively at the rest of the class. "Not like these."

Ignore him, I think. Don't take the bait. I answer the question for them, push on to the next one: *If Mamadou worked on his resume, he _______ get a job cleaning toilets at the church.* We're actually hoping to employ Mamadou this way. But, out of irritation or sheer stubbornness, I read out again, "If Ahmed worked on his resume . . ."

Ahmed grins mirthlessly, wags a finger at me. "Ah, my friend, I see. I see you."

"I think is . . ." Tareq begins, "could?"

"Excellent!" I ladle on the encouragement. "Molto bene! Fantastico!"

Ahmed claps sardonically. "Good, good. Star student, very good answer."

Tareq looks both hurt and confused. Older men—Ahmed has twenty years on Tareq—are supposed to command, and bestow, respect. When Ahmed first started coming to the center, he had a little group of acolytes. He bragged he'd been all over Europe, had even gotten into the UK, where he'd worked for ten months at a kebab shop run by a distant cousin. Plenty of guys wanted to know how such a miracle had been wrought, even if we were constantly telling them that trying to ride the top of a truck through the Chunnel, as Ahmed claimed he had, was suicide. He got deported, of course. Soon enough, he undermined himself here. He told everyone he was Afghan, but all the Afghan guys said he spoke Farsi like an Iranian. And the Iranians insisted he was Pakistani, knocking him even further down the ranks of who did and didn't qualify for asylum. He said he'd been everywhere. He just ended up coming from nowhere.

"What you want, teacher man?" he says to me now, grinning wolfishly.

I break away from him, write on the board, *If Mamadou could go home, he _______ help protect his parents from the war,* and start to read it aloud.

"No," Ahmed says, "you use my name."

"I thought you didn't like it."

"I give you my persimmon."

I don't conceal a laugh. "Fine. 'If *Ahmed* could go home, he blank help his—"

"No."

"What now?"

"My parents. My father, he sick. My mother, she dead."

This brings me up short. "I'm sorry."

"What, you kill her? She old. Why you always say sorry?"

"Okay, sorry. I mean, well . . . Let's just . . . Tareq?"

"Ahmed would help his parents!" Tareq answers. "I want help my parents too. If I get job, I save them too."

"Good!" I say. "Excellent! Excellent use of the first conditional!"

"Bravissimo, bravissimo," Ahmed mutters. He leers at Tareq, his face twisting up as he claws at his calf. He just told me his mother's dead in a voice like he was reading from the paper, like it's all just someone else's sorrow. I glance at the clock. Twenty-five minutes till I can jump on my bike, escape this stinking place, order my first prosecco on the Piazza della Madonna di Monti. I scan my worksheet, see how far we have to go, and skip ahead.

"Right, the third conditional," I begin. "Okay, so we use this to talk about things that *might* have happened in the past . . ."

Even for a native speaker, third conditional is tough: things that did or did not come to pass, how life might be different if they had or had not. I write out the formula—past perfect, past participle—go over it three times. The guys blink back at me. Ahmed grimaces like the Bocca della Verità. I've jumped to the hard stuff, I realize, to catch him out—to remind him that there are things, many things, that I understand and he does not. I write on the board and read aloud, rapid-fire: *If Ahmed had known there was no work here, he _______ gone home to his country after a year.*

"You know the price to come here?" he says. "Home? No, never."

If Ahmed hadn't been fingerprinted at Lampedusa, he could have _______ for asylum in Germany.

He bats the idea away. "Ich hasse es, Deutsch zu sprechen!"

If Ahmed hadn't lost his mobile, he _______ asked for the girl's number.

"Why I want call woman? Already got enough problem."

If Ahmed had married a European girl, he _______ received citizenship.

"Then I go out of Italy, my friend. I go!"

If Ahmed had studied English harder, he _______ be so lonely.

"Lonely?" he says. "How I could be lonely? Ten roommates. Six hundred people in my camp. My friend, I'm not lonely."

Ahmed's acolytes—a quiet, fierce-looking group—used to gather near the prayer room to play chess. Just by the tone of Ahmed's voice over the chessboard, I could tell he was bitching: the shitty camps, the endless trays of rice and egg and reheated pasta, the Carabinieri always hassling you for your documenti, the Americans always smiling and telling you, I'm sorry, I'm sorry. Over winter, Ahmed and the rest of them grew out their beards. People started whispering that they were Talib, they were Daesh. It scared us. Just like that our community could become a haven for the disgruntled, the radicalized.

Then the weather got warm, and Ahmed's buddies took off, probably to pick tomatoes or melons in the south. When his flock departed, so did his beard—he looked even older than before—but our mistrust lingered. The Afghans and Pakistanis froze him out, and he wouldn't stoop to socializing with Africans. He was always sitting in the chess corner by himself, waiting for someone to come along and play.

"My friend, my friend," he says now, "what the cheapest way to Paris?"

"I don't know," I say gruffly. "Why should I know? Let's focus, everyone."

Maybe Ahmed wouldn't feel so guilty about his mother dying, I write on the board, *if he'd _______ home and looked after her.*

There. Let's see how he likes that one. First conditional: for things likely to happen, for what's possible. Second: to make plans, to dream dreams, even nearly impossible ones, and chase them down. And the third conditional: for the things we rue, that we wish against all wishes had been different, for the crushing weight of all of our regret. It's language that it might actually help Ahmed to learn.

But Tareq, of course, jumps in. "If Ahmed gone home he looked after her."

Ahmed scoffs. "Bravo, amico. Bravo."

"If I were you, Ahmed," I tell him point-blank, "I'd hush up about now."

Even the beginning students hear the sawtooth in my voice. They fall even more silent. The fluorescent lights sizzle above us.

Finally, Sarwar pipes up: "What mean, 'If I were you'?"

"If I had your life," I explain brusquely. "If I were in your position."

Watchful, bewildered expressions all around.

"If I were you. We use this to give advice. These are the things *I* would do."

"You tell me what to do?" Tareq ventures.

"No, no, you don't *have* to do it. It's just a suggestion. Advice."

"What mean 'ad-vice'?" Sarwar asks.

"It's when I . . ." God, I'm struggling, casting around for the Italian, not finding it. "It's when I *suggest* something." Why am I even here, and not out where I so easily could be, *should* be, enjoying this beautiful city? I'm thirsting for that first prosecco, but all I can taste is Ahmed's fucking b.o. "It's when you don't *have* to do something, but it'd be good if you did. You see? It's like, shit, what's the word for—"

"Consigli," Ahmed translates. "'Advice e consigli.'"

"Ah, certo!" Sarwar says. "Consigli! Io so."

Ahmed flashes me another strained grin. Was he waiting to step in, enjoying watching me flounder? I stumble through the next question, leave some words out, accidentally write in the answer to the one after that. Then Ahmed's phone starts dinging again.

"Turn that off, please," I say through gritted teeth.

"Un momento."

"Turn your phone off."

"It my friend. He in the jail."

"Because he's a guard. I get it. Very funny. Turn it—"

"No, he really in the jail."

"Ahmed, turn it off *now*."

I'll kick him out. No, I'll ban him from the center altogether. Why let him back in? He'll just keep making trouble. Ding. Some you can never reach. Lost in the desert, stranded at sea, they'll take the water you offer, spit it right in your face. Ding. Ahmed becomes every refugee, every dark figure looming on our doorstep, engorging our fears, getting our most craven demagogues elected, making the truly vulnerable suffer along with him, making it so we, even if we have everything, simply can't afford to open our hearts. Ding. Not to everyone. No, never to all of them. Even if every last goddam one is a bona fide victim or—ding—"Ahmed, would you just"—ding—"Fucking Christ, Ahmed, get out, just get—"

I stop myself. Outside, I hear the low, shabby din of the rest of the center, the muffled voices and cries. The clock ticks like a bomb. The guys sit blinking at me. Ahmed makes a show of turning off his phone.

"Would you?" he murmurs, abashed for once. "What this?"

"It doesn't matter," I say roughly.

"Would you help me?"

"What?!" I all but bark out. "What is it this time?"

"No, this my question. Would you help me? This conditional?"

"It's polite." I have to push way down to calm myself. "A polite way to say something. To ask for something."

"But where the 'if'?"

I scrawl on the board. *Would you help me (if you can)?* "The 'if' is implied. It's there," I say. "But it's not there."

Not a great answer. But Ahmed seems pleased. "Yes, good, polite. Very good." He starts humming to himself. "My friend, when the singers begin?"

"What singers?"

"They tell me famous singers. From America."

"I don't know. Look, we're nearly . . . Let's just—" The last question is still up on the board: *Maybe Ahmed wouldn't feel so guilty about his mother dying if he'd _______ home and looked after her.* I just write in the answer then quickly rub it all out.

"What mean 'looked after'?"

"Never mind, Sarwar. We're done, everyone. Finished. All finished now."

The guys file out. I don't have the energy to explain to Sarwar. A domani, I tell him. And he'll be here tomorrow, and all the days after that, even if he never gets anywhere. I nod to Mamadou as he goes out, slipping back into French as he rejoins some other Malians. We're trying to find him a new camp. But tonight he'll sleep outside again, curled in on himself, remembering that first boot to his ribs, bracing for the next one.

Tareq lingers, hoping for some extra tutoring. Maybe one day he'll become a waiter. Or open his own restaurant. A shop, a hotel. He'd be the perfect refugee—educated, eager, deferential—if he were actually a refugee. Economic migrant. Truly, that shouldn't matter. Yet, today, I just don't have it in me. I wipe off the rest of the board, start straightening the desks. Tareq tries to help.

"It's all right," I say impatiently. "Non grazie. A domani, a domani."

Out in the common room, it's borderline chaos: the clatter and shouts around the foosball table, the rumbling of some dubbed action movie playing in the TV nook, the undifferentiated roar of fifteen different languages all clamoring at once.

I'm ready to leap on my bike and fly away to Piazza della Madonna di Monti. I'll get a few pages written before Rob, Danielle, and Jessie join me, to get drunk and loud like all Americans abroad, reveling in the ease and power of our shared, globe-stomping language. I'm about two seconds from getting out when Ahmed catches my eye. Fuck.

"My friend, my friend, you don't like my jokes?"

"Listen, sorry," I say, again. But, then, how can I even trust that his mother's really dead? "Anyway, sorry about the—"

Ahmed waves it off. "You stay for the singers?"

"There are no singers."

"No, the singers, the singers. Look."

He points to the cluster of college kids Rob was showing around earlier. They've dispersed to the ping-pong and foosball tables. A few are playing with the guys. I see their T-shirts now. *Whiffenpoofs of Yale, A Cappella A-Round the World, Spring 2017.*

"Famous singers," Ahmed says. "From America."

A famous college a cappella group wouldn't be enough to make me cross the street (or maybe to the other side). But, okay, they're here to ease the gloom a little, to distract the guys from the boredom, the ceaseless grind of just roaming the city day after day. I look again at Ahmed wearing his long coat in the June heat and realize that, despite what he said about an overcrowded camp, he too is sleeping rough.

"They want to sing," he says decisively, "they sing."

As if on cue, the kids turn away from their games and congregate at the front of the room, swinging into place with aw shucks grins, as if they all, well, howdy, just happened to find one another here. "Today we've got a great treat, a great gift for you all," Jessie says. "A wonderful performance from our friends," Rob says. "All the way from Connecticut, gli grandi cantanti, il Whiffenpoofs!"

The basses start up some doo-wop thing while the others vocalize around Billy Joel's "Uptown Girl." A few of the guys glance up from foosball or their phones, but most seem uninterested or simply exhausted. Ahmed, on the other hand, is staring at the Whiffenpoofs with glee.

They go for the chorus—"Uptown gir-*lll*, you've been living in your white-bread world!"—and Ahmed starts clapping along. Then he does a few steps of some Middle Eastern dance, a wild grin stretched across his face. For a moment, I see a flash of a much younger man, a man like Tareq. He makes a few more turns and lets out a loud, startling whoop. The Whiffenpoofs smile appreciatively, if stiffly, and a few even try to join in with Ahmed's dancing. For a moment I'm weirdly jealous; music knots strangers together faster than any language. Then Ahmed turns to me, and his face drops back into its familiar, inscrutable mask.

He comes over and says in a low voice, "They sing for money?"

"No, it's free. They're here performing for free."

"Ah, so they have money. They take piety on us."

"Huh? Oh, pity."

"Yes, yes, pity."

"No, they're here for . . ." But I don't really have an answer.

"What you do for money? How much they pay you teach here?"

"Nothing. I'm a writer."

"I see, I see. Maybe you write my story, make some money?"

"Don't worry. Refugee stories aren't selling. They say they have all they need."

The Whiffenpoofs hit a final crescendo. Then, abruptly, the song and dance is over. Ahmed crosses the room again to shake all their hands. "Would you help me?" he asks each one in turn. "Would you help me?" Rob catches my eye and gives me a thumbs-up that, somehow, depresses me more than anything.

I gather my things for a hasty exit. But I find myself drifting toward Ahmed as he too is leaving. He lobs a desultory "You got five hundred Euros?" at me.

"If I had it," I say, lying, "I'd give it to you."

"Ah, so there always 'if.'"

"Sure," I say. Then, as if out of nowhere, "What's up with your leg?"

Wincing, he pulls up the cuff of his baggy wool trousers. A big chunk of flesh is missing from his calf, the wound healed weirdly, twisted around the remaining muscle and bone, mottled all gray-green and purple. For a moment, I forget the clamor around us and stand there staring at the wound. With a last grimace, Ahmed pushes down his cuff.

"Arrivederci, amico," he says, seeming embarrassed.

"A presto, Ahmed."

I shake hands with him, put my hand over my heart, watch him limp up the stairs and back out into the tourist-thronged streets. Then I go out and unlock my bike. As I whiz through the crazed traffic on Via Nazionale, I see him for a moment, hitching his leg down the cobblestone sidewalk. And then he's gone, just another face in the crowd. I draw in the electric air of the city, and I pedal harder and harder.

WEATHER ENOUGH

His younger brother died young. Late on a February evening, on a county road heading for Chicago, speeding toward a party in the north suburbs, he and his best friend Mason plowed into the broadside of an eighteen-wheeler. Forty minutes outside of Kishwago, there were already seven empty beer cans rolling around the floor of the BMW. Mason was driving, and John, when Tim tried to picture his brother in the moments before the accident, would've been handling the music and rolling joints with the little machine he always kept on him.

Tim had been living in the city the last three years, temping and renting a garden apartment on Western Avenue. After the call from his father, he sat staring at the linoleum in his living room, only startling out of it when the couple upstairs started shouting at each other. When he got out of the taxi at Union Station, it finally took form. *Killed on impact*. All the way to the end of the Northwest line, those words kept hammering through his thoughts.

The following Saturday, he stood with his father in the funeral home. The guests came in red-cheeked, stripping off coats, hats, gloves. Their hands, when Tim shook them, felt chapped and cold and full of bones. The receiving line kept going. Parents, teachers, well-wishers from the community. High school seniors, friends of John's and Mason's, uneasy in suits meant for homecoming or graduation. Pretty girls, tanned even in the winter months, two or three of them old girlfriends of his brother's. Tim reached out to take the next hand—it was warm, sweaty—and then he recognized Hayden Kersch, Mason's older brother.

"Hey, buddy," Hayden said. "You holding up okay?"

It had been maybe five years since he'd last seen Hayden, around the time John first fell in with Mason's circle of friends. Hayden had been tagging along then, wearing his hair long like the younger boys, dressing in polo shirts, baggy khakis, and boat shoes. He was twenty-six or twenty-seven now, his hair the same butter blonde but cut short on top and buzzed on the sides. He wore dark blue trousers and a blazer with golden, anchor-shaped buttons.

"We're okay," Tim said, "We're doing okay. I'm sorry about Mason too."

The Kersch family had held a private service for Mason the day before.

"How you like it down in Chicago?" Hayden said. "You like it okay?"

Tim hesitated. "I might be coming back awhile. Back to Kishwago."

Hayden smiled, a big, uninhibited smile. "That'd be nice, buddy. That'd be real nice. Me and John were close, Tim. We were real, real close."

Though Hayden had dropped out of Kishwago High the year Tim started, he'd heard the rumors. Hayden had been caught, twice, in the girls' locker room. Someone had painted "PEDO" on his locker in Wite-Out. In Diverse Learning, he'd asked Cristina Enriquez to prom, and she'd turned him down, what a creep. Tim hated small-town gossip. It was one of the reasons he'd gotten the hell out of Kishwago. But that didn't stop him from going careful with Hayden.

"Yes, right, I—" he answered haltingly. "He mentioned you."

"You like basketball, Tim?" Hayden said. "The Bulls? I'll have you over some time. Got a new TV. Satellite hookup too."

Tim's father leaned over from where he'd been talking with one of John's teachers, rested a hand on Tim's shoulder. "We'd better keep things moving."

"If you guys need anything," Hayden began, "I really . . . I'd like to, just, anytime . . ." He didn't finish, or couldn't, and, still smiling, went into the next room, where, surrounded by flowers, photos, and mementos, John's pine-and-brass effect casket sat like an altar.

Tim told his temp service he'd be out of town, emergency leave. Maybe a couple of weeks, he told them, then sublet his garden apartment for a month. Back in Kishwago, he and his father silently ate their way through the casseroles, platters, and dips neighbors had dropped off after the funeral. It snowed heavily two days in a row; they rose early to shovel the drive, then did it again. At night he sat up listening to his dad's Neil Young and Steve Miller records on headphones. The needle bumping into its run-out woke him from dozing, and he blinked back to the world, confused where he was, listening for the clamor of traffic on Western Avenue.

After that first week, his father had to go back to work. He did stamper maintenance on contract at a tool and die up near Elkhorn, just keeping ahead of the mortgage. When Tim had the house to himself, he went up to John's room. He sat on the bed, let his gaze wander over the Milwaukee Bucks and Chicago Cubs posters—Kishwago was right between the two cities—the X-Men trading cards and *Sports Illustrated* swimsuit pages John had tacked to the walls. Tim picked up a Little League trophy from the dresser. Not more than a few pennies' worth of plastic and wood, yet it suddenly seemed holy. It had taken his dad more than a decade to finally throw away Mom's clothes, to move her gardening books and knitting things to high shelves in the spare room. John had been too young to remember her, but Tim bore the image of her wasting away in the cancer ward through several very quiet years in grade school. The house had already felt like a mausoleum, and now, Tim understood, John's room would become its inner sanctum.

He walked into town and had breakfast at a little place known for its Swedish-style pancakes, murmuring thanks to the handful of old patrons who came up to say their condolences. Otherwise, town felt hushed, emptied out. Down in Chicago, Tim often saw brochures for Kishwago: lakefront condos, sprawling mansions, the town square with its ice cream parlors and antiques shops trading in old Coca-Cola signs and decorative butter churns. During summer, weekenders from Illinois tripled the town's population, but come Labor Day most of the big houses sat vacant. Tim left half the pancakes uneaten, paid, and set out on a long ramble along the lakeshore path, walked until the moon came slowly out, making the thick frozen lake shine dull and cloudy, like a cataract eye.

When the calls started, Tim barely noticed. The house phone would ring around seven or eight, after dinner. His father would answer, murmur a few brief apologies than hang up. Sales calls maybe. But one evening, Tim heard his father say, "No, he's out. On a walk somewhere. I don't know where he goes." The next evening, halfway through a taco casserole, his father pushed his plate away, fixed Tim with a searching look, and said, "Don't get mixed up with that Kersch boy. You got enough to think about without those people adding to it."

From what Tim knew, the Kersches had money—a family real estate fortune—but were careless with it, living high and running up debts. At the pancake place, he'd overheard the old gossips saying that Mr. Kersch was already out in California again, Mrs. Kersch back in her second condo, down in the Loop, sobered up just long enough for Mason's service, and that there was already talk of them having stiffed the funeral home on the bill.

Tim took his plate to the sink, scraped it down the disposal. "Don't know why I would," he said over the churning blades. "Guy's dealing with his own stuff."

Early the next afternoon, Hayden showed up on the doorstep.

They'd just been driving around for half an hour, down by the lake, out into the corn, soy, and mustard fields that hemmed in Kishwago on three sides. "We could go over to the diner," Hayden was saying. "They got great pie at the diner." That was the other breakfast place in town, the late-night one, where all the high school kids went.

"Right, sorry," Tim said. "Just haven't been hungry."

"It's cool. No worries, Tim. Hey, what do you like to do down in the city?"

When Tim left Kishwago, it seemed he was escaping, getting even somehow with his birthplace. But in Chicago he was just another face in the street, the offices where he temped, the handful of web design classes he'd managed to take. "Museums," he said. "Read a lot."

Hayden turned to him, grinning. "What if we just got coffee at the diner?" Though his clothes looked freshly pressed, there was still something rumpled about Hayden, like he himself had been left out to dry and badly ironed. "They let you just get coffee."

"Sorry," Tim said again. *Killed on impact*. "Just not in the mood for people."

They wound up at a lakefront condo building, not the one where Mason had lived with Mrs. Kersch, the little she was around, but a shabbier place where most of the units got rented out to weekenders on a budget. Hayden led them up to his apartment, a series of practically bare rooms with a corduroy couch and armchair, a huge entertainment center, a broken ping-pong table, and old takeout cartons, soda cans, and pizza boxes in the kitchen. John had always referred to this as Mason's "other place." Or anyway, this was where they went to hang out and get high when Mrs. Kersch was in town and she and Mason were warring.

Hayden sat down in front of a paused video game. Some martial arts fighting thing. "You can unlock all of the fatalities in this version!" Hayden said.

Tim settled back into the couch. It smelled of dust and pepperoni.

"Want to try, Tim? Versus? Story mode?"

"You go ahead. I'll watch."

"Everyone missed you around here." Hayden started clicking buttons. "It's great now you're back. Real great."

The characters hitting and kicking each other on screen rumbled from large speakers flanking the TV. Tim reached for a can of Old Style from the twelve-pack he'd bought on the way over. Before he knew it, he was seven down. Hayden was drinking Mountain Dew, clicking ever more furiously, winning match after match. Tim's phone vibrated with incoming texts, but he didn't look, knew they'd be from his dad, asking where he was. "Listen . . ." Tim said foggily after the eleventh beer. "I gotta, really . . . Get a ride back?"

Streams of their breath filled Hayden's car. It was a convertible, luxury fifteen years ago, never meant for winter. Hayden put the heater on full blast and took the south-shore road, which skirted the lake then ran out through some low hills. Though the night was clear, the winter sky seemed close on top of them. Off to the right stood the darker mass of a larger, flat-topped hill.

"Hey, Tim," Hayden said, "let me show you this one thing. Just real quick."

Well, what was he rushing home for? The beer was finally warming him up. He had a long night ahead either way. "Okay," Tim said. "Real quick."

Hayden turned off on a gravel road. It pocked against the undercarriage as they climbed, then turned to bumpy, hard-frozen dirt. Bare sumacs growing up between tire ruts brought them to a stop. They got out and walked, and as they came to the top of the hill, Tim realized where they were. Spider. John had talked about it all the time. Bonfires, kegs, weed, acid, making out, getting twisted. Tim could see the power lines angling over and down the sides of the hill like spindly legs. The center of the clearing gave a view over the town and lake. To the north, Tim could make out the snowy undulations of a golf course and a sprawling building alongside it.

"Look, Tim," Hayden said, pointing, "the Playboy Mansion!"

The magazine had once been headquartered in Chicago and had chosen Kishwago as the bucolic site of their first grand getaway, way before all the starlets in the grotto out in LA. Everyone in town knew this, but Hayden still proudly explained it all. Tim listened to the breeze rattling the long, thin branches of a stand of white birches at the edge of the clearing. As Tim and Hayden crossed toward them, something took shape, a curved triangle, ten feet high, silhouetted against the grey sky. It ran back into a dark mass, thirty or forty feet long, an old motor yacht leaning on one side of its hull, most of the fiberglass bottom having caved under the boat's weight.

"The fuck did this get here?"

"Don't know!" Hayden said happily. "Someone ditched it." Then with reverence in his voice: "Once everyone slept by the fire, and John's shoes melted!"

Tim ran his hand along the cold hull, his senses reaching out for John's presence. They'd been two years apart. Even in the crowded middle school cafeteria, he and John used to eat lunch together, just the two of them. On weekends, they'd flip through X-Men comics at the drugstore, spin out their own elaborate stories in that fantasy world, shy but content, even proud, not to talk to the lakefront kids, the ones who wore designer jeans and drove German cars to school. Then, in his freshman year, John suddenly came into his own, tall and athletic and popular with girls, out with his new pal Mason four, five nights a week. Hayden's strangeness hadn't stained Mason. Or, anyway, Mason was good-looking and constantly threw parties. Either way, Tim wanted nothing to do with any of it. He was already pointing himself at Chicago. After graduation, when he took the train home on weekends, he hardly saw his brother. Now and then, Tim, John, and their dad would sit at the dinner table in delicate silence. John was sleeping through most of his senior year, had come home a couple of times in a cop car. Tim could feel their dad vibrating with worry but never commented, too afraid to touch that worry.

A long, slow wind rattled then swayed the birches. Tim hunched into his coat. His eyes had adjusted to the dark now, and he saw that the intact half of the hull was covered in graffiti. "Hey, buddy!" Hayden's voice rang out above him. "Up here!" Hayden had managed to climb up into the cabin of the boat. He wedged himself into the driver's seat and began to spin the wheel one way and then the other, making motor noises.

Tim called up to him, "Got a lighter?"

Something thumped softly on the snow, a square, metal Zippo. He felt the warmth of Hayden's hands on it. By the light of its flame, he could just make out the graffiti. *Jessie N gives head. Class of '93! Dare to say No. BITCH.* These ancient idiocies made him desperate to be away from this place, but he lingered, examining them as if they were hieroglyphs, clues to what had become of his brother.

Finally, they wove back down to the convertible. "Want to come over tomorrow and watch basketball?" Hayden said as they drove away from Spider. "We could see a movie. There's the diner. They let you hang out even if you just get coffee."

Tim didn't answer. He was concentrating hard on the beer sloshing around his stomach, on not puking it up. When they turned onto his street, he told Hayden, "Don't pull in. My dad goes to bed early. Don't want the lights to wake him." They sat on the side of the road with the heater blasting. The long icicles hanging from the gutter glowed faintly at the outer edge of the headlights. "Well," Tim said, "take it easy then." But the thought that he'd now have to lie awake and drunk in bed with his thoughts, *killed on impact, killed on impact*, was unbearable.

"Remember?" Hayden said. "How John liked music? Pearl Jam and all them?"

"Right. Sure. Of course."

"Yeah," Hayden said softly. "Can't even listen to those CDs now."

"I'd better split."

"Want to watch the Bulls tomorrow?"

Tim looked again at his iced-over house. "Fine. Pick me up at five."

Through the front door window, he saw his father sitting at the kitchen table staring at a half-eaten plate of something. Tim had always regarded his father as a man who simply endured bad news and good alike, but since the funeral he'd looked constantly startled, like he was waking up every minute and still finding his younger son gone.

"I had to get out," Tim said as he swayed in. "Walked down, looked at those new condos they're putting up over on Button's Bay. Anyway, yeah . . . bedtime."

His father inspected his plate of hamburger mac casserole. "Sleep safe," he finally said.

By mid-March, the last of the cards reading *condolences* and *sympathies* had arrived. His father stowed them all in a Tupperware on a high shelf, just below the gardening books and knitting things. The weather got warm, a brief thaw, then it was hard cold again, the streets and sidewalks etched with the quick-frozen crosshatch of tire treads and boot prints. Tim started growing a beard. Fewer people seemed to recognize him in the grocery line and at the gas station.

Most nights, Hayden would pick him up, and they'd go over to his place and play games or watch basketball. When the Bulls came on, Hayden sat wringing his hands, calling out to the players on screen, "Come on, get that board. Get it! Offense, now. Let's go. Let's go!" He turned to Tim. "Ever go and see them, buddy? When you were living down there?" He hadn't. "My dad and I went once. Saw Jordan. Awesome. In the summer, I'm going out to California. My dad says we'll go see the Lakers."

Tim got another beer from the fridge, rolled the can across his forehead. This was already the fifth or sixth time he'd heard about this trip to California. It occurred to him to ask questions about the Kersches. But he didn't have it in him to feel for such people.

They went to a few movies. Hayden's place was starting to feel like being sealed up in a jar. "Anything," Tim said. "I don't care." The movies were all loud and badly acted and featured borderline offensive jokes. Afterward, Hayden breathlessly recounted the action scenes.

"They jumped off that building and *survived*?" Tim said, unable to resist a little mockery. "You think someone can strap on a parachute midfall?"

"You can do it! I saw these guys on TV. Totally insane."

"And, what, they were already wearing the chutes under their business suits?"

"They got all *kinds* of stuff we never know about. The Stealth Fighter, Tim. Remember about the secret Stealth Fighter? That secret came true."

"Shit," Tim said, "give me the laws of physics at least!"

He laughed out loud, for what felt the first time in weeks. For a moment, he was lost in the movie's world, the same reality he'd imagined on the afternoons he and John spent reading comics. He looked at Hayden, his still gleaming eyes. "Fine!" Tim said and laughed again.

But that night in bed, he lay sweating and turning, trapped under a heavy quilt, hearing John's voice, John mumbling a joke, the two of them just goofing around, nonsense jokes, knock, knock, John's mouth moving, mumbles, no words, sweating, turning, the front door opening, who's there? Dad's leaving, going to work, the screen door banging shut, come on, what's the joke? tell me, tell me—and then he woke, fully woke, feverish, twisted up in the quilt, to the sun kaleidoscoping in through the frost-starred window, to a quiet like thunder.

The diner was small and brightly lit with nicotine-yellow Formica tables and bitter, scalding hot coffee. Tim and Hayden were in the booth in the very back, Hayden talking about California, the Lakers, Venice Beach, cruising around in his dad's Porsche 911.

Tim broke in, "Where's your dad live out there?"

"Santa Barbara. Me and Mason go see him when it starts getting nice out."

Tim thought to correct him, but just then the waitress brought them plates of eggs and corned beef hash. "Okay, well, does your dad come out here much?" Tim didn't know if he was trying to be interested or cruel. He could see Hayden squirming. "When did your folks split up? When are you visiting him again?"

"He comes here sometimes, for his business. He'll bring me out there soon."

"You don't know when?"

"Me and Mason go out to California every summer. Or in the spring sometimes. We always see the Lakers."

The waitress came back, refilled Tim's coffee, Hayden's root beer. Tim was half-drunk and jumpy, had the dazed feeling of sliding and rising out of himself at the same time. "Hayden," he said deliberately, "you're talking in the present tense."

A strained look came over Hayden's face. He was sitting up stiffly, holding his pop with both hands. "Hey, we could go swimming at my mom's clubhouse."

The bells tied to the door of the diner jangled. Four high school kids pushed in from the cold. Three boys in khakis and puffy coats with ski hill passes pinned to the zippers. A petite girl with dark hair and dark, glinting brown eyes. As they took a booth in the front window, Hayden waved to the girl. She waved back, hesitated, then came over.

"Hey, Jessica!" Hayden said. "What are you guys doing?"

On first glance, she was the kind of girl Tim had never been able to talk to in high school. On second, her worn-out jeans were not deliberately so, and her carefully applied makeup concealed a spray of acne. "We were just talking about Mason," she said. "About how much we miss him. How are you doing, Hayden? Holding up okay?"

Tim was trying to remember if he'd seen her at the service for John. There'd been so many people. Whichever way, she didn't seem to recognize him, thank god. Such was the outpouring of community support he'd felt like a guest at his own brother's funeral.

"Doing good!" Hayden answered, so eagerly it made Tim shrink inside. "You all up to anything fun?"

"The guys just got done with hockey," she said, gesturing back at her friends.

"Who won?" Hayden said.

"Oh, it was practice."

"Hey, you all should come over to my place. We got beer. We can party."

She looked back at her booth. Her friends gave her an uncertain wave. "Well, it's . . ." Tim could see her make the same calculation he had. "I've got a wicked calc test tomorrow. Maybe some other night?"

Hayden grinned back at her tightly. "Sure! Whenever!"

"But I wanted to say I've been thinking about you, hoping everything's okay."

"It's cool, Jess!" Hayden said cheerily.

She excused herself with a gentle smile. Tim murmured, "G'night," relieved that he hadn't needed to introduce himself and get into another round of condolences. A hush seemed to have fallen over the diner, the cars and trucks buzzing through the slush outside suddenly louder. Tim and Hayden sat with their coffee and pop, and the girl and her friends ordered pie, two separate islands under the fluorescents. Tim watched some court room drama on the TV above the counter. Finally, the other group paid and left.

Hayden and Tim wandered out in silence. They walked to the lake, a little inlet that served as a slip for putting in boats, and down to the gravelly beach, where they picked up stones and tossed them out onto the ice, skidding them till they disappeared with a gulp. Forty feet out, they could just see a buoy bobbing in a little lagoon of free water with a distant, slapping sound. They started aiming their throws, but neither could hit it. "Come on," Hayden said under his breath. "Come on, come on!"

And then he was out on the ice, running out toward the buoy, hurling stones as he went. He slipped, fell backward, landed heavily. Even thirty feet away, Tim could hear the water in the ice seething to the surface. By the weak light above the boat slip, he tried to make out where Hayden had fallen. "Hey, Hayden!" He listened for a reply, for movement or breathing, and heard nothing. "Hayden! You okay?"

Tim stepped out onto the ice, went out twenty feet, then dropped to his belly and crawled. Under its slushy surface, the ice was hard and sharp. He numbly felt it bruising and scraping his hands. The front of his coat soaked through, then his shirt. His skin was burning with cold. "Hayden! Fuck, Hayden!" He bumped something with his foot—he'd almost gone right by—Hayden lying on his back like he was gazing up at the stars, an oddly peaceful sight.

"You awake? Hey!" Tim twisted around, grabbed Hayden's shoulder and shook him. Hayden stirred. He grasped the back of his head and rubbed it, then pushed himself up to his knees. The ice squeaked and popped all around them. "Don't!"

"It's cool, it's cool . . ." Hayden reached to give Tim a hand up. The ice under their feet seethed but held. Hayden turned and walked calmly back to the frozen beach.

His father was already in bed, snoring fitfully. Tim hauled himself upstairs and into John's room, stripped off his wet coat and clothes, and crawled into John's bed naked, shaking, hands squeezed under his armpits, prickling with pain as sensation returned.

Five weeks since John had died. Watching his mother pass had been no preparation. *Killed on impact.* Or only enough to harden him now, so that what he felt—regret, anger, resentment, giddiness like mad laughter—was just one solid, immovable block. He lay there, temples thudding, blood hammering through him, just as out on that ice his whole body had thumped with one impulse: *Live, live.* But Hayden had acted like it was nothing, no danger, the ice wouldn't give way, the frigid water wouldn't swallow just you. Tim was warm now, sweating even, but he shivered all over again.

In the morning: his father calling up, the screen door banging shut,

Tim still shivering in his brother's bed, only getting up to piss. The sun came up, went down, came up. He didn't bother to look at his phone, but he could hear the texts and voicemails vibrating it. That afternoon, or the next, someone clumped up onto the front porch, knocked too many times, then went away.

Finally, his dad came up, sat on the corner of John's bed. "Figured you were sleeping off another hangover." The old man had grown out his mustache. The little they'd seen of each other in daylight, he hadn't noticed. There was a bit of fluff stuck to it.

"Been sick," Tim said, voice sticking in his parched throat. "Okay now."

"Couldn't make it to your own bed? Or were you trying—" His father started to say something more, then changed directions. "Hungry? Want some dinner?"

Dinner? Jesus. He'd lost track of the day completely. "No, I need to get out."

"I'll get my boots."

"Don't know how far I'm going," Tim said.

"I'll keep up."

At the shore path, they walked in silence, cutting across the long lawns that ran up to the lakefront homes, past stacked-up boards from the piers taken out for winter, boathouses and gazebos humped over with a late snowfall. They stopped to look at a four-car garage that had been added to one of the bigger houses. "They finally got that done," his dad said. "Know the guy who did the work. Took those flatlanders for a ride."

"I guess I'm one of those flatlanders now."

"You just lived down there."

"Well, that is the definition."

The night was still and mild, and they had pocketed their gloves and hats. His father reached up, ran a hair through his greasy, unkempt hair. Neither of them had really gotten back to the world. "No need to get sharp with me."

"I've been trying down there," Tim said. "Fuck if it's going anywhere."

"There's work at the tool and die. Contract, no bennies, but it's work."

How could Tim explain? Apprenticing with his father, living in the mausoleum . . . It wasn't that he felt himself too good for this life. Hell, he couldn't even get through night school. It was that the clamor of the city distracted, soothed him even, made him forget the death that clung to every molecule up here.

"Nice night for a walk," his father said when Tim didn't reply. "Ground stores up heat. Right around midnight's best part of the day."

"I haven't been trying to abandon the family."

"Never thought you were," his dad said. "Never wanted to keep you boys on a leash. Let them run, right? That's what they say. But I had dreams about it, even before it happened. An accident. OD maybe. Dreams where you just watch it happen, powerless. But I never was. Just couldn't rein him in. Your mother would've done better." His father crossed his arms over his chest, as if trying to keep warm. But Tim saw his shoulders trembling. "You don't have to answer anything to that. I'm just speaking it."

They went further down the shore path, climbed a set of wooden steps, came to a lookout. The lake opened out below them, the cataract eye. On the opposite shore, Tim saw the dark curves of the hills, the powerlines spindling down the side of Spider.

"Only ones guilty are that truck driver, that little shit Mason, his fucking parents."

"Don't know who's to blame," his father said after a time. "But I saw it coming."

On the walk back, it began to rain. "Great," Tim said, "now this."

"I don't know." His father's voice seemed to float delicately on the crystalline night. "Feels okay. Weather enough, anyway, for a breath of air."

The next morning the rain had eaten away half the snow. Tim

watched through his bedroom window as the sun melted the rest. He picked up the phone, dialed Hayden's number.

"Hey," he said, "there's a party tonight."

They walked up the hill through the sumac and scrub, Tim carrying a thirty-pack of Old Style, and came out into the clearing. The boat hulking out of the gray evening seemed monolithic, eternal, even if it was just junk. In its lee were the remains of a firepit. Tim turned up two hewn logs to sit on—"We're early"—and cracked a beer.

"Yeah," Hayden said, opening a Mountain Dew, "things don't really start till later." His expression was solemn, almost ruminative. The snow had been melting all day, but the ground underfoot here was still hard, not yet turning to mud.

"Bet its eighty degrees in California." Tim finished his first beer. "They're all on the fucking beach smoking joints." He tossed the empty can into the pit. "Come on," he said. "We need a fire."

They found dry needles for kindling at the base of a stand of pines, took up fallen branches, pulled strips of papery bark from the birches. Hayden worked eagerly, running back and forth to the firepit. By the time they had a good pile, they were both sweating and red-cheeked. Tim cracked another beer. He'd lied to Hayden about there being a party, but now he half-expected it himself: teenagers clambering up the hill, shouting, laughing, the *shush* of ice sliding around in their coolers, their cigarette cherries dancing through the night. He'd envied John not remembering their mom, not knowing that weight, whooping it up every night, not thinking twice, him and Mason getting into that car already half-drunk... But, no, John had only felt the weight differently. He hadn't wanted to be their father or his older brother, all frozen up inside, too afraid to thaw.

"Still got that Zippo?" Hayden handed it over. Tim knelt and touched the flame to the kindling. The wet wood started hissing, then the larger chunks caught. Hayden hunched over, staring into the fire, his eyes reflecting pinpricks of its light. To Tim, it seemed he was in some other place, not on that hillside waiting for a party that would never happen but in the past, Mason still there, his mother, his father, all still at home. They were all around him, waiting just past the firelight.

"When's everyone get here?" Hayden said softly.

Tim imagined hurling burning chunks of wood off into the night, against the boat, the hollow hull booming, its fiberglass drooping and deforming, all of Spider going up with it, torching the whole goddamn town. Instead, he just waved his fingers through the dying flames, watched the embers going dark, the wood too wet to burn long.

"You can make some other friends," he said, not looking at Hayden. "Someone who likes basketball, videogames. Someone more like you."

"You like basketball, Tim. You like games."

"You shouldn't hang out with high school kids though."

"Me and John and Mason used to come up here all the time." Hayden's voice wavered over the last of the flames. "I miss them. Me and John were close, Tim. We were all real close."

"No," Tim whispered, "you weren't." He rose from kneeling, looked off toward the dark undulations of the golf course, the resort that had once been the Mansion, the endless expanse of flat, glaciated prairie beyond. "He's gone. He's a million miles away."

With the toe of his boot, he scattered the fire.

Back down in the city, he rented an even smaller apartment in his old building and after two months of interviews, gave up and temped again, data entry, down in the Loop. A parking spot came up for rent, and he bought a used Camry. He went on a few dates with an older woman from work who chided him for being so silent all the time. Life seemed something like it had been. He was dreaming about John less, but the dreams, when they came, felt realer than waking.

That July, he got a call from his father, one outside their terse weekly check-ins. No one had seen Hayden in more than a month, his father said. The mailman, when Hayden's box started filling up, had knocked on his door, found it unlocked, the condo vacated. Calls went out to Mr. and Mrs. Kersch, but it'd been news to them. The police had contacted Tim's father, who was asking, in turn, if he'd heard anything. "No," Tim said. "Nothing. Zero." He didn't say that he'd blocked Hayden's number, saw it as part of moving on.

It took another ten days for answers to arrive, and then it was in the local paper. Hayden's convertible had made it as far as Oklahoma City before breaking down. He'd checked into a Super 8 on his mom's debit card. The next evening a party had erupted a few doors down. Some locals having a blowout. Hayden, apparently, had introduced himself. What happened next had yet to be determined, but the state police said that Hayden had withdrawn eight hundred dollars from a nearby ATM and that there had been several unsuccessful attempts to do the same early the following morning. When the maids smelled something two days later, they ignored the "Do Not Disturb" sign, went in, and found Hayden with the covers pulled over him, his body splotched head to toe with bruises. Internal bleeding, the coroner had concluded. The purpose of Hayden's journey remained a matter for speculation, but when Tim mapped the route, he could see easily enough where it was aimed. Southern California.

He went to a bar that night, played pool by himself, half watched a Cubs game on the big screen, dozed with his head on the bar. When he ordered another Old Style, the door guy came over. "Time to go, chief." Tim wouldn't budge. The man took him by the shoulder, yanked his arm behind his back, hustled him out.

"Don't you tell me!" Tim shouted. "Don't!"

When he found his Camry, he was a long time fumbling with his keys. He stabbed at the lock, missed again, and with a squeal of metal on metal, scratched the key against the door. A couple coming down the street crossed to the other side. He made another scratch, scored it white through the paint. And then another. Another. Reeling in the street, key in hand, he set to it.

THE LINE

My father's voice, I begin there. Raspy, deep, quiet. Tata worked for twenty-five years refinishing hardwood floors and never wear a mask. His voice sounded to me like that soft leather, you know . . .

"Like what?" Cindy leans into me on the couch as my fingers twitch and I tear up the label on another Zywiec. We have the news on mute, all this stuff again about the kids they lock up near the border. "Oh," she says, "you mean suede?"

Exactly. Exactly like this.

Early that morning, his suede voice whispered, "Danek, Danek, wake, please. We are late. Already late." I rolled over, said I don't want to go again. I was fourteen. Sleep was a palace. Finally, he got me up—brush my teeth, comb my hair, shirt, tie, slacks. Why did we need to dress up for such things? "When you meet the government," he told me, "you dress good."

In his pickup, I sat with my feet up on the belt sander. The streets were empty—we lived way out past the airport—but Tata drove five below the speed limit, like always.

"You can go fast," I said. "It's not a funeral."

He looked over, hurt, then saw me working my fingers.

"Relax, Danek. Relax, okay?"

One hour later, we arrived downtown. Now I'm there every day, I hate it. Back then, I was twisting my neck up to see. We got a spot far from the Federal Building. "Diabeł!" Tata said, grinding the curb parking. "Ah, to hell . . ." Then we quick marched through the gray dawn streets, until we finally turned onto Jackson. Tata swore again. The old brick building took up one whole block, and the line already went around the first corner, the second corner—we ran—the third corner too. That was where we got in. In front of us, there was a Mexican family, parents, a daughter maybe my age. Behind us, some old Indian couple. After them, ten, twenty, forty more people got in, the line going around the fourth corner, as well, tail eating head.

"No worry," Tata said, breathing heavy. "Plenty time. Goosey loosey, okay?"

I looked up and down the line, at all the hundreds of people waiting. It was July, already hot at seven in morning, everyone already sweaty, nervous. The Indian man turned to look at us. He wore a blue polo, white pants. His wife: white linen dress, big straw hat. They had an actual picnic basket. "Good morning," the man said to us, "can we offer you some breakfast?" His wife held out some pastry in wax paper.

"Thank you," Tata said, a little confused. "But we're having maybe hot dog later."

That didn't stop them telling their life stories. The line did this to people. Her, a lawyer. Him, a psychologist. They met in college in Evanston, always thought they would go back to Delhi, maybe London. The worst thing for them here was the loneliness. Then their boys were born—one a chef now, one also a lawyer—twenty-five years go by, and, well, they all just stayed. "This is the land," the husband said with a big grin, "where your mother-in-law can't just stop by for tea." His wife swatted him, said they were here for their final interviews. For citizenship.

"Ah, congratulations," Tata said, smiling shy. "Big news."

Uncle Abram helped us come over when I was ten. He had the flooring business, helped us get visas. One day, citizens—that was the big dream. My father's big dream anyway. Tata, Mamo, they fit together like tongue and groove. But she was homesick. She only had Tata's family here, and all they talked about was hardwood, tile, laminate, vinyl, linoleum . . . Back in Gdansk, she was a teacher—geometry and calculus at the polytechnic—but the only work she got here was cleaning houses. "I am so bored," she used to say, "I do equations in my head all day." Every immigrant story goes like this. My parents write the check, so one day I cash it.

"Danek," Tata said, "goosey, okay?"

I stopped clenching, shook my fingers, like getting water off. But I felt Tata tense too. Ahead of us, the Mexican guy was smoking, apologetic, blowing into the air above him. Tata was trying to quit. At night he coughed and coughed—all the sawdust he breathed—but pack of smokes still vacation for two bucks. The guy finished his, dropped it in a Ziploc in his pocket. Blue jeans, western shirt, cap that said "Lutz Family Pork Producers." His wife: blouse with roses on, elastic waist pants. Poor, quiet, keep to themselves. Like any Mexicans you saw around.

Then I looked at the girl.

Cindy wrinkles her face when I say this about Mexicans. But now she laughs, teases me. "Ah, so *that's* where this is going," she says. "A love interest and everything."

I dry my hands, touch her leg, little tickle. "Second most beautiful girl I ever saw."

She laughs again, my favorite sound. "Fourteen-year-old boys, they never grow up," she says and moves my hand up to her waist. Like the counselor tells us, make all touch meaningful. "I didn't know that," Cindy goes on. "About your mom being homesick."

Mamo, Tata, I tell her, they still had the old way: loyal to family. Uncle Abram did a lot for us—even if he took eighty percent of the profits—and Tata honored that. But for Mamo, my uncle was another reason not to stay. Once I got caught cheating on my English test, and Uncle Abram told me, Don't worry. The test is cheat. Make your own way. There were reasons, I tell Cindy, he had all the flooring business on the far north side. "Tata could've started his own crew, down south. But he never would. He never stepped forward himself."

"Hmm," Cindy says, maybe question, maybe pleasure. I let my hand go up her belly. We've been talking about a baby. "Okay, really," she says, "was the line *that* long?"

"This the nineties. Every form, stamp, signature—you have to get them in person. Can't do it all on internet. You have to get in line."

"If you're trying to make all of this metaphorical . . ."

"What metaphorical? This was actual line. And before we come over, six years for visa."

"I know, honey. I recognize that. But what I'm saying is—"

"Look," I say, "you want to know how long we wait? I tell you."

Nine o'clock, that was when we finally started to move. On the front side of the building, they'd opened the door, let a few people in. Tata and me, first time we came downtown, we didn't know about the line. We came at opening time, didn't even make it inside the building. Second time, we arrived an hour earlier, but it rained. We actually got to reception, soaked, and they just said we had the wrong stamp, come back some other day. On the third time—

"Hang on," Cindy says, "weren't you telling me about the girl?"

Okay, I tell myself, just relax. "Diabeł, right, the girl . . ."

As we all shuffled forward, the sun rose above a big church across the street and caught the tips of her dark hair, made them glow. She wore jean shorts, a tie-dyed T-shirt, a backpack with buttons and patches sewed on: Varsity Volleyball, Jazz Choir, National Honor Society, "Jessica" circled with hearts, a smiling alien head. Sticking out the top of her backpack was a big envelope with the INS seal. She took it out, fanned herself. Her shirt moved, showed her belly button. I couldn't help leaning forward, to stare closer.

She turned to me. "Hey," she said, "want to play a game?"

"Huh?" My tongue went fat in my mouth like a big ham.

"I'm Jessica."

"Yes, I know, I— I'm Danek. Polish," I blurted. "Here for my green card. Fourth time we come here."

"Amazing! We're here for mine too. Are you excited? It's trip number eight for us." I couldn't answer her question. She talked really fast, like always catching breath. "Yeah, eight times down here!" she said. "You see, the problem is, we keep having a problem with . . ."

Her status, her papers. Chiapas, they left when she was two. Her dad worked at a big pig farm, her mom as a maid in a fancy hotel by a lake. First grade, they put her in slow English, though she had zero accent. She tested right out, all A's since, even when she was taking care of her sisters. Well, one B, eighth-grade gym—the white boys all yelled, "Aye caramba!" as she ran down the soccer field—though what was the point of A's without papers? No papers, no financial aid. But then her quiz bowl team won state finals, at the big university, and a professor there wanted to sponsor her. The timeframe was crazy—green cards took six months, at least, to process—which was why today was so important. They had to get the scholarship application in, and they'd planned to get down here way early, but the bus never came. They'd called her cousin. His car wouldn't start, so they had to get a different bus, and now . . . She gestured at the line.

"I like her," Cindy says. "She sounds like a huge nerd. And, Christ, to think we're still failing kids like her so—"

"I don't know," I say. "She make me feel . . . embarrassed."

I try to explain: I was awed of this girl. But, also, annoyed. My grades, except for math, stink. I never lose my accent. And the jokes—Polaks screwing in light bulbs, Polaks falling out of trees, Polak firing squad stands in a circle—they make them about us too. I hear them all.

"Well, look," Cindy says, "you can pass. It doesn't define your every waking moment."

"Pass for what?"

"It's all evened out." She waved around, our beautiful house, three bedrooms, one for nursery, white oak engineered floors that last a hundred years. "America made it up to you."

"Okay, okay." Because I went to city college, worked whole way through. Now I do insurance tech, make algorithms for everything, enough to pay for all this, house, two cars, vacations up north, everything Tata always dreamed about. "So why I have to feel guilty for that?"

"Not guilty," Cindy says. "Aware maybe."

"Where you think these jokes come from? The guards at the camps. Hitler told them in his speeches. They teach all about the Jews here, but everyone forget about Polaks."

"Danek, it's not a competition."

"Not for you, I think."

She has a look on her face. But she tells me, "Okay, I'm listening. Listen first, listen first." Something else our counselor tells us. "You were playing a game?"

The line was moving. Not fast but moving. There were carts selling coffee, doughnuts, churros. All overprice, but what can we do? Maybe half the line was Mexican. Also, Africans, Chinese, Vietnamese, Arab, some Polish like us, Russian, Albanian . . . The sun was getting heavy. The Indian couple had their straw hats and magazines like you saw at doctor's. Tata finally broke down, bummed a smoke from the Mexican guy. The Indian man wrinkled his nose, but Tata just said, "Muchas gracias, amigo." Embarrassed, I started flicking invisible water off my hands again. No, I told myself, not in front of her.

To stop, I asked Jessica about the game. She explained the rules: We point out people in the line, name them, say where they come from, what they do for living. "See him," Jessica said, "down at the end, the super tall guy?" An African in a white dress shirt. "His name's William. He, um, lives down in Dalton. And he works at . . . a bank! He's a drive-through teller."

"Eh? How you tell?"

"His shirt, it's pressed." It was. "But his pants are wrinkled." Yes, also. "When he sits in his little bank booth, you can only see his top half. So he doesn't care about his pants."

She smiled, so bright I blinked like mole.

"You're just guessing," I said.

"Yeah, so that's the whole point of the game."

"Okay, maybe her?" I said, pointing to a potato middle-aged woman with a page of newspaper tent over her head. "That's . . . Maja." She reminded me of crazy lady who lived in the park back home. Her name was, okay, Maja. "From Gdansk."

"No, where she lives *now*."

"She's from . . . Waupaca, and she has, uh . . . cat business?"

A year after my mother died, Tata started to see this woman with a kind of pet washing service. She always had cat hair on her clothes, but she was nice, pretty. They went out five times, and, once I heard them laughing downstairs while they listened to old Czesław Niemen ballads. But, then, Tata just stop calling her. Three weekends in a row, he took me to the cemetery. The flowers he brought were bigger than the slot in the wall with Mamo's ashes. They wouldn't fit the holder. He kept trying, they kept falling out. "Diabeł!" he shouted and turned away from me. But I saw: He was crying. He wouldn't even let me see him cry.

"Maja," I went on, "she give your cat bath for, I don't know, five bucks?"

"Cheap for a cat bath!" Jessica said, talking fast, breathless again. "They scratch you. They go crazy in water. Once I was out by this lake, and I saw a cat trying to . . . Sorry, I . . ."

Jessica stopped talking. Her eyes went hazy. She tilted forward, her eyes fluttering, then reached out and put her palm right on my chest to hold herself up. My heart exploded like a landmine. She leaned away, sorry, sorry, fluttered her eyes again, and started the game back up.

"Donnie"—she pointed out an Asian guy in paint-spattered jeans holding hands with a woman in a sundress—"he paints houses over in McKlusky. But he's also an artist. On the weekend, he and his girlfriend go to the park, and she reads in the grass while he paints her. Sometimes, when he does a house, he finds a place where the owners never look, and he paints her there. The ceiling of a closet."

I laughed. "Behind fridge."

"On the tops of the cabinets!"

"Tops of ceiling fans!" I say. "Under hardwood floors!"

Jessica laughed too. My heart detonated again. "Okay, him!" A Russian-looking guy leaning against the wall, yawning, blinking in the sun. "Sergei, from . . . Twin Oaks. He, um, tests mattresses for a bed company?"

"Right, a professional sleeper!"

"He gets in trouble for being wake on the job."

Tata and her parents watched us, not understanding but all smiling. Every immigrant story like this: Parents must learn, kids just know. I thought Jessica and me, we still might say where people really come from, but she only said nearby towns and cities. And the jobs—no one was scrubbing shit toilets, not like Mamo, not like Jessica's mom. But the game, it started making the line move. Twelve-thirty, we were already on the second side of building. More carts were out: hot dogs, burgers, bottle water, Snapple. The mood was good, everyone happier to wait, happy for the thing they were here to become.

But as we got closer, I felt my fingers tense, start to ache.

"Okay," I say, flexing them now, thinking maybe more ice. "Okay, yes," I tell Cindy, "so let me explain third visit. One before this one."

That time, Tata and me, we got into the line around six, inside by two in the afternoon, then past the guards, past reception. The line went up two flights, people standing on the stairs. Then, in the waiting room, they finally called our number. We went into an office. Inside were two men, one with red hair, one bald like an onion. Onion pulled down a screen, took my picture. Red sat me at a desk, brought out an inkpad, a box of baby wipes. He took my thumb, pressed it into the ink, moved it to the card with little boxes.

"A roll," he said, "just a gentle roll."

I did what he said. It left a smeared mark. He frowned, had me wipe my fingers, ink them again. "Okay, relax," he said. "Relax your fingers." But the next card he crumpled too. "Again." The one after that I just left a big smudge on. "All right, come on, relax already, okay?"

I looked up at Tata. He looked at the clock: five to four. Quitting time. "Don't worry, Danek." His voice was soothing but also panic. I looked down at my hand. Relax your fingers—what did this mean? How did you even do that? I could only think to wiggle them a little.

Red laughed—"Now he's got it"—grabbed my hand, shoved it into the ink, then studied the card. "No. Again." The clock ticked past four.

"Shake 'em out," onion said. "Try that."

I did what he said. They felt more relaxed, maybe. But the fifth and sixth prints were worst. Red gave up. "Okay, folks," he said, "come back some other day." Tata was smiling at me, but he looked like when the doctors said about Mamo's cancer, like at the cemetery when he stood crying at that little slot in the wall, the only thing he could give her at the end. He was never bold. He could never take the step to be real provider. Maybe if he made more money, we could've afforded some real healthcare, best hospital, best doctor, best—

"Don't be so hard on him," Cindy says. "Your father was a good man." She got to know him the year before he died. His heart went before his lungs did, clenched up on him in the middle of the dairy aisle at Jewel-Osco. By the time I got to the hospital, he was gone.

"Yes, he was good," I say quietly, "but he was not . . . making decisions."

"Indecisive," Cindy says. "Indecisive. You know that."

"Right, right. He promise Mamo one thing, Uncle Abram another. Can't please everyone." I take Cindy's hand. "But I want to give you everything I promise."

She leans over, kisses me. I tense up again. But she keeps holding my hand.

"You were just nervous that day. You had a hundred reasons. Here, try this." She lets her fingers go limp in mine, soft like little bird. "Go ahead," she says. "Try."

But I can't. Not yet. I need to tell her the rest, to say what happened.

It was past one o'clock. The sun weighed like a slab, the asphalt burned, the one Porta-a-John they put out for us was buzzing flies. We waited. The INS agents must have been on lunch. I felt the whole line thinking *go*—all of us *pushing* everyone ahead of them, hating them for being first.

Slowly, slowly, we turned the corner, onto the front side of the building. There it was: the door. Not the final destination. Not the office with redhead and onion. But, still, the door! Around it, there was a big brass frame. And around that, paintings, murals: fields of wheat and corn, proud factories puffing white smoke, proud workers turning their faces up to the shining sun. Even then, I knew that America had not been this for a very long time. Still, that door—it was triple high, triple wide, like everyone could get inside.

Of course, there were guards. Two guards letting people in one group at a time. They went slow, stingy, and at two o'clock, they stopped letting anyone in. If you weren't inside the building by two—there was still one hour to get up the stairs, one hour in the waiting room—no chance of getting into the office.

As we waited, people were also coming out. Either they'd arrived very early, dry-eye and hollow-stomach early, or they could afford lawyers to make a special appointment. Some came out excited, hugging, high-fives. The front of the line clapped for them. Others came out confused. They'd glance back at the door a few times, then just drift away. That feeling—it went all the way down the line, made everything go tight as wire. People started pulling out their paperwork, checking, double-checking. Jessica pulled hers out too. But she just started fanning herself with it, fast.

"Hey, look," I said, pointing out an Arab guy in a white golf visor and khaki shorts. "He has factory. Where they make . . . little golf pencils! Like at the putt-putt and . . . Hey, you okay?"

She leaned against the building, in the little shade it cast. The fanning was making her shirt ride up again. I saw that she was outie. Then I looked up at her face. She only smiled, a faraway smile. The game was over. There was nothing to do. I squatted, paced, clenched, and unclenched my fingers. Tata was reading over my papers, holding them up close to his face, like that help him understand, sweat from his forehead splotching the forms. I watched his eyes move over the words, puzzling over them. He kept blinking against the sun, and it was like his blue eyes changed color with each blink: deep blue like Masurian Lakes back home, sad blue like when he told me about my grandfather and Katyn Forest, hard blue of bodies piled in a ditch, ice blue like starvation after the war, trembling blue like leaving Gdansk, like the day Mamo got diagnosis, serious, official blue like American passport, like the sky the day of my mother's funeral when—

There was a big clatter. Suddenly, someone was shouting. "It is frozen! This hot dog, it is completely frozen!" The tall African, our drive-through bank teller, was cursing one of the food vendors. "You expect me to pay six dollars? For this hot dog? Disgusting, very disgusting!"

The vendor spoke back at him in Spanish. One of his condiment containers had tipped over and was oozing yellow-green relish all over the sidewalk. The African got angrier, chopping the air as he said again,

"Disgusting!" He maybe spent months, years in some refugee camp. Now here he was, screaming at a hot dog vendor. The line also did this to people.

I could see Tata wanting to help. He always wanted everything fair. He told Uncle Abram to pay the other guys on the flooring crew the same as our family. He tried to get him to stop cheating on taxes. He didn't like the way he went around the northside, taking down his competitors signs, and sometimes doing worse, much worse. Those murals around the door, Tata could believe in them. A good world for all—he was waiting for it to come. But around Uncle Abram, he always backed down. He never broke away, started his own flooring business down south. He just kept taking his smaller share of the profits. He would go on waiting forever.

Now, he handed me my papers, stepped toward the African guy and hot dog guy. But then he stopped, turned back around. Something else was happening. I turned too, and saw Jessica on the sidewalk. Her mom was kneeling next to her, whispering fast in Spanish. The Indian man knelt too, laid the back of his hand on Jessica's forehead. "She's burning up. Heat stroke," he said. "You need to cool her down. Is there somewhere nearby with air conditioning? Do you understand? Can someone translate?"

The mother was looking around for a place. This was business district, nothing open Saturday. Someone said there was a Dunkin' Doughnuts, maybe four blocks away. Jessica's mom and dad talked in Spanish. Everyone else stood watching, except for the African guy, who was accepting a free hot dog and continuing, almost friendly now, to scold the vendor. The vendor offered a bottle of water, and Jessica's mom gave her sips. Then her dad got his arms under her, got her off the sidewalk. "Hey," I said, "you okay?" Jessica gave me a weak smile, then let her mom take her by the elbow and out of the line. Her dad stood watching, face twisted up like pierogi. He turned to Tata. Tata touched him on the shoulder, like he was saying, My heart goes out for you. He offered Tata another cigarette. Tata smiled sad, waved it away.

Jessica's fainting, everyone felt it. Up and down the line, people were whispering, sweating, watching the door. It was after one-thirty now. The Indian man said to Jessica's dad, "Poor girl, but she'll be fine. Young people bounce right back." But her dad didn't answer, only nodded, said, "Thank you, thank you."

"Jesus"—Cindy takes my hand and squeezes it—"that poor family."

Yes, but it also reminds me, I tell her, about a time Mamo fainted.

This was the October when I was thirteen, when they said she had till maybe Christmas. My mother, she'd been in bed for so long. We wanted her to see the leaves, the fall leaves all exploding color. But she slept most of ride. The one time we woke her up, she just smiled and said softly, "Piękny, Danek. Piękny." It meant beautiful, and I wished it had been. But my father had waited too long again. Most of the leaves already gone.

When we got her back to the apartment, she fell. Her legs just went out. We got her inside. Then she peed herself. We helped her to the bathroom, and she got undressed. But she was too weak to get in the tub. So, Tata, he bathed her. I stood outside the door, worried but also embarrassed to see my mother naked. I heard Tata singing to her, that old Czesław Niemen song "Allilah." Now I sing a few bars in Polish.

"What does it mean?" Cindy asks.

"He's telling a girl he'll come back," I say. "God willing, he'll come back to her."

I don't say what I'm thinking: That, if we never left Gdansk, maybe my mother would not have died. I understand that cancer is in the blood, not from the stress and worry from moving to this country. But, here, it is so hard to say where the line begins or ends, where you stand in it, if your neighbor is friend or stranger, if you are really just waiting, alone, for nothing. In Poland, you have to wait for the doctors too. But, if we had stayed home, Mamo would've had her own family to help her—her sister, aunts, many cousins—not just Uncle Abram and his fat crazy kids, not just her afraid and confused husband and her American stranger son.

Tata finished singing Czesław Niemen, fell quiet. And then he called my name. He told me to come in, he needed me. I had to hold her up, her wet, naked body, her gray paper skin against mine, while Tata dried her with a big towel. Then we got her back to bed. There were tears all over her face. She looked Tata in his blue eyes, said, "You were not wrong. You were not, you were not . . ." She said it again and again. She wanted him and me to understand, to remember it wasn't our fault. But I always think that it was.

Cindy squeezes my hand tighter, but I'm still far away, looking up at Tata, watching him watch Jessica's dad, who kept leaning out of the line, looking, looking. I shook out my fingers again.

"Loosey, Danek," Tata said, rough-soft. "Loosey."

Thirty feet away, only a few people were going inside. Only every six, seven minutes—the security guards were picky because of time. We were all so close. There could've been shoving, fights. But everyone was just staring at the door, those fields, factories, big gold rays of sun. It was nothing like where we stood now. Melting asphalt, Porta-a-John fumes, boiled hot dogs—the smell was all in my face, making my fingers ache even more. Jessica's dad lit a smoke, took two nervous puffs, stomped it out. He leaned out of the line again, looking back, forward, everywhere. And then he turned to Tata.

"Please, to . . ." He searched for words. "Here, you keep my . . . Please, if I . . ."

"Go," Tata said. "We are here. Go find them."

Jessica's dad took off running. His cap fell off at the end of block, but he didn't even stop to pick it up. Another ten minutes went by. My fingers felt like they were in a vice. The guards were barely opening the door now, and they checked their watches every time they did.

"Relax, Danek." Tata looked up and down the street. "Relax . . . Diabeł! If they don't—"

"All right, folks," one guard said to Tata and me, in that friendly cold way Americans say it: *folks*. "You two, go ahead. Go ahead now."

Before Tata could answer, the other guard stepped out on the sidewalk, so everyone could see, and waved his hands over his head. "Last ones, folks! Two o'clock, time to go home!"

People far back in line turned away, grumbling, angry. Just behind us, they held on to their places, still hoping.

"We open again Monday, nine o'clock!" the guard shouted. "Don't call. We don't pick up the phone. Sorry, it's time. Time to go home and—"

"Excuse me, sir, excuse me!"

There was a flurry of feet and voices. Jessica came running up, her mom and dad just behind. She looked so pale. She had to lean on her dad to catch her breath. Her mom and dad started talking to the guards, fast Spanish, confused English.

"*No más*," the guards said, "*no más*, folks." They turned to Tata, ready to end their day.

But my father, he hesitated.

"Dan," Cindy says. "Please don't tell me . . ."

I'm quiet. "I don't know," I finally say. "I don't know words to explain."

Cindy makes a sound.

"What?!" I say.

"Her scholarship. You could've come back another—"

"You don't know how long! We waited too. We hurt too!"

I heard two voices. Tata said my name, softest leather. But I heard Uncle Abram too. *Make your own way*. So I stepped forward. I tried not to see Tata's eyes, Jessica's eyes. I looked away from the Indian man and his wife. She gasped, he whispered something. I heard Jessica's parents still begging with the guards, the guards not understanding. *"No, más. No, más . . ."*

Then I was through the door and inside the cool marble hall. A few moments later, Tata also came inside, his eyes down as third guard waved a wand over us. Tata kept wetting his lips, about to speak something. The day that thick plastic card—it wasn't even green—came in the mail should've been our big day. Instead, he just pushed it under my bedroom door. He never did say anything about it.

Except, just before we went into the office with redhead and onion, he touched me on shoulder. I thought, for some reason, he wanted to apologize.

"Dad, it's okay," I said. "I'm ready."

I shook out my fingers, clenched and unclenched a fist.

Remembering it now, I do the same. Cindy looks at me, worried, confused. But I feel better. For the first time since all this news from the border, I feel loose. Our counselor was right: Cindy and me, we need to listen, we need to touch. I reach for the remote, turn off the TV. I touch her belly. It's cool and soft. My fingers draw slowly along her skin.

"Hmm," she says and shivers. "So, that's all you have to say?"

"I don't know the words," I tell her.

"You do!" she whispers, hard but far away. "Damn it, you do. You just pretend not to."

"No," I say, suede voice like Tata. "But I want to. I want to show you."

Touching her belly, my fingers stiffen again. And she pulls away.

AT THE CENTER OF THE SAILING WORLD

I

On all but the coldest days of that year, the neighbors could see him taking his wife for a walk. She was loved. Neighbors, colleagues, students, strangers in the grocery line or public library—no one in the small lakeside town had been able to resist the chatty little Englishwoman who'd taught history at the high school. When she opened her mouth and that canorous accent came pouring out, people had listened with smiles on their faces. They'd asked indulgent little questions about Princess Di and taking tea, about double-decker buses, rain, warm beer, and what it was like for Susan and Lomax living in this tiny place out in the middle of the cornfields.

Every afternoon at four, Lomax could be seen leading Susan down to the lakeshore path, holding her hand, sometimes going ahead and waiting patiently for her to catch up. She came dawdling along, stiff-kneed, lurching. They continued slowly on, Lomax nodding hello to their lakefront friends out on their decks and patios, Susan staring straight ahead, expressionless. What she had recovered since the stroke was largely this—her mobility, the ability to swallow, point to things she wanted.

Six months in, the doctors and therapists told Lomax the window for further recovery was closing. Still, they said, she was young. Only fifty-four. There was a chance. Ten months in, in the wake of two smaller strokes, she began to lose what she had regained. The rest of her time she spent in bed with Lomax at her side. He'd all but given up work at his boat and sail company. He hadn't been to the yacht club in months. In the first of Susan's final days, they had regular visitors to the house. It was too much for Lomax, seeing these kind people already grieving over his wife, speaking softly to her and asking questions as if she could respond. He started keeping the curtains closed, the phone off the hook. As the months wore into summer, days went by and the only faces he saw were the boy who delivered the groceries and the hospice nurse who came in the afternoons to change Susan's sheets and give her a bath.

The service was long. So many people came to the podium to remember Susan—her vivacity and intelligence, everything she'd done around the village and for the community, all the stories from her classroom, her voice, her laugh. It was an entire catalog of a lost woman. Lomax, sitting center in the front row, had to smile and nod through it all. Susan's relations hadn't been able to afford the airfare to come across for the funeral. Lomax had offered to pay, but they wouldn't accept. He'd already agreed to send over half her ashes for a memorial in Bournemouth. As for his own family, only his older sister, Geralyn, came. He held her hand through much of the service. On his other side sat Top, his business partner, and Top's wife, Linda. Afterward, everyone seemed to linger, hesitant to say a final good-bye. Lomax waited patiently until the last handshake, the last hushed condolences, until the door finally closed behind the last guest.

At home that evening, sitting on the screened porch with glasses of beer and white wine sweating down their sides, Top and Linda half-asleep on the wicker love seat, he buried his head in Geralyn's shoulder and sobbed into her blouse.

"Come on, Max," she said, gently scolding him. "It's over now. At least it's over."

He was fifty-two, broad across the shoulders and chest, with a full head of thick brown hair and placid blue eyes. Over the past few years, he'd begun to wear the kinds of clothes that middle-aged men, no longer trying to counterfeit their youth, wore to hide the crest of their bellies—golf clothes, business casual. But when Susan had been bedridden, when it was rare that he ate a meal large enough to fill the sink with dishes, when he seemed tired all the time and came down with a snuffling cold every other week, the old Lomax had been carved out of him. His jawline reemerged, the concavity of his cheeks, the wings of his collarbone. He found himself having to dig around in the attic for his old shirts and trousers. At a cost, he was more the man who had crewed all those champion boats than he'd been in ten or fifteen years.

After the funeral, Geralyn stayed on for another week, a strange reminder of home: Ditchling, a quiet village on the South Downs, where Lomax hadn't spent more than a fortnight since age seventeen. He'd been a quiet, aloof boy, had failed miserably at school, then worked for a year at a baker's rolling out the dough for sausage rolls. On not much more than a bored whim, he'd moved to Brighton, found a job at the marina, and quickly discovered a talent for sailing—an agility and sureness on deck, a sense for subtle shifts in weight and wind that he'd never felt on land. He came into his life almost without trying, and in his twenties and thirties traveled the globe crewing in Grand Prix races: Antigua, Honolulu, Newport News, Port Huron, the Isle of Wight, Mackinac, Bermuda, Bahia. He held no particular allegiances. American, Australian, Kiwi boats—he'd gone wherever the money had taken him.

He met Susan in a bar in Auckland. Petite, outgoing, impulsive Susan. Three years older than he was, a wild girl, as she said herself back then, who liked a drink and a snog. She'd quit a job in London to go backpacking for a summer with two of her girlfriends. When the girlfriends left for Tasmania at the end of that week, Susan stayed behind. The first time she saw him, she later told Lomax, with his sunglasses, sun-bleached hair, and tan, she'd thought he was American. The girls were completely gone on you, she said. Lucky me, though. Very lucky me. The two of them lived an itinerant life together, Lomax flying off in charter planes for races, Susan waitressing in whichever port of call they'd made a temporary home.

A call came one day from Top, Lomax's skipper on the America's Cup boats and the closest he had to a best friend. Top was moving back to his hometown to start building sport boats. Kishwago was a place you could grow to love, he said. Lomax told him it sounded like the absolute middle of nowhere.

"More than nowhere," Top said. "Wisconsin. More cows than people, and so much corn they give it away on the side of the road. How many years of competition you got left, Max? Two, three? Bow out gracefully. The way the world works these days, we can run this thing from anywhere on the globe."

For fifteen years, Top and Lomax built and sold several hundred boats a year, their renown growing steadily, good fortune following good fortune. Their company brochures referred to Kishwago as the "center" of the sailing world—a joke on the town's flyover obscurity and a winking acknowledgment of their successes despite the fact. Lomax continued to travel as the public face of the business, his catalog looks, mellow Sussex accent, and laconic demeanor speaking to their customers of everything that went along with buying a "Top 24"—effortlessness, sophistication, entry into an old guard of sportsmen and gentlemen.

The surprise was how readily Susan settled in Kishwago. She went to a university in Milwaukee, got her teaching certificate. In the community, she ran the garden club, took over the traditionally male task of organizing the Venetian Fest fireworks. In their fifth year in Kishwago, Lomax and Susan bought their lakefront home. Susan got herself a cat, a secretive calico that wandered off for weeks at a time. Lomax had the company shop build him a little play boat, a thirteen-foot dinghy he named *Elizabeth*, and they used it in the summers to make the short trip between their pier and the yacht club. When they became citizens—they'd wanted to vote Reagan back in—they hung a Stars and Stripes from the mast, just under Saint George's Cross.

Lomax stood with Geralyn in the international terminal at O'Hare. In the week following the funeral, she had busied herself receiving visitors to the house, taking in the platters of sandwiches and sliced fruit, the pies and cookies, keeping everyone entertained out on the patio, serving them tea in the June heat. In that brief time, she had been as big a hit as Susan, and several people, having forgotten that Geralyn was Lomax's sister, commented on the likeness.

"Quick good-byes," she said at the security point, her shoes already in her hands. "Norman and I will see you in a month or two, won't we? Your nieces would like a visit too."

He mumbled something about how much he had to do around the house, Top needed him back at the office, the last of the orders for next summer, a regatta they were sponsoring . . .

"Come home for a week at least." Geralyn stood up on her toes and gave him a kiss on the cheek. "Susan wouldn't want you going to ground on us."

He lay on top of the sheets that night, too exhausted to get up and turn on the AC. The silence of the house floated depthless above him. If he lay there shouting and screaming through the night, no one could possibly hear him.

At three in the morning, he found himself down in the entertainment room, where his trophies, cups, and plates lined the shelves on three walls. With the windows open, he could hear the constant swelling thrum of cicadas, the sloshing and gulping of the waves against the pier. He found a rag and a bottle of polish. There was only the faintest patina on each piece, but it was tedious work, and by sunup he wasn't half done. He sat slumped on the sofa, dreaming he was out searching the woods for Susan's cat.

The yacht club was a grand affair for Kishwago. It sat snugly in the center of Button's Bay, gleaming in its stucco white, bearded with a long, immaculately tended lawn that ran down to a narrow strip of beach and three wide, white piers. A massive bronze anchor sat in the center of the lawn, a relic salvaged from the wreck of an old trading ship at the bottom of Lake Michigan.

On a few occasions, Lomax met Top and some other sailing friends at the club and stayed for an hour or two drinking Foster's. The other men were in their twenties and thirties, drank heavily, and only wanted to hear Top and Lomax talk about cup racing. The days and weeks spent living in the bubble of an ocean cruiser, existing on dehydrated food and no sleep, knowing the exact stink of everyone onboard, every physical and mental tic, the way eight men wove together through the rush and clamor of a sprint, main sail booming, cranks ratcheting and whirring, every back straining to keep a boat balanced on a knife edge . . . Lomax felt so distant from that time; it was only by deadening effort that he could drag up details of a particular race. Without Susan nearby—even when she'd been across the room with her own friends, it bolstered him, made him confident, talkative—he suddenly found the male company at the club distasteful and tiresome. He'd heard all their jokes, and their stories often seemed like depressingly familiar iterations of his own. All of the past seemed now like the same endless race.

But even more than the men at the club, it was the women he wanted to avoid. He knew how American women, especially, responded to him. He knew a furtive, appraising glance by now. He was too quiet to be a charmer, though everyone had always seemed to expect that from him. Marriage had come as a relief. He'd proposed to Susan three months after they met.

He fell into a solitary routine, working around the house in the morning, jogging or riding his exercise bike in the afternoon. He looked in at the office once or twice a week to check on a handful of boats whose progress interested him, but the thought of dealing with customers was too much. If he went to the club, he went early and had dinner alone on the balcony, where he could look out as the setting sun bled into the rippling mirror of the lake. The waitress who worked Tuesday and Thursday nights, a pretty girl about nineteen or twenty, hardly had to ask for his order. Chicken Florentine, small salad, two, sometimes three pints of Foster's.

One evening, he found himself staring out at the waves, the big willows nodding at either end of the little beach, the anchor bulking darkly against the short green grass, its wind-polished edges reflecting the setting sun. The world was tidy and well burnished. He lingered with a last swallow of lager in his glass, feeling somewhere between satiated and utterly miserable.

The waitress came up, asked if he was finished, took his plate. She stood there another moment, hesitating. She was a small, wiry Mexican girl, her black hair worn back in a tight ponytail, her dark complexion making three tiny pimples on her forehead stand out brightly. She stood there with her water jug, looking down at him with a stormy expression, annoyed or confused, he couldn't tell which. There were no other customers in the restaurant. A couple of boys in polo shirts and white shorts sat at the table farthest from Lomax drinking Cokes and wrapping silverware in cloth napkins.

"You're from England, right?" the girl said in a rush.

He only nodded yes and smiled politely. He thought he must have looked truly pathetic if she felt obliged to talk to him.

"Someone said Ireland or Australia."

"No, you've got it right."

"There was this other English person I met once, this woman who came to my school and gave a talk?" She said it like a question, asking whether he knew her.

Lomax remembered the big box of slides Susan had lugged around to some of the grade schools in the county, the little speech about their peregrinations she'd practiced in front of him one night in the kitchen. "Where did you go to school?" he reluctantly asked the girl.

"Delevan."

"Then that was no doubt my wife."

The girl's expression brightened. "I asked if she'd ever met the queen. I was only ten; I wanted to know."

The moment arrived when he ought to have told her that Susan was gone, that familiar dance—the explanations, the awkward apologies and murmured sympathies—that always seemed to leave nothing to say afterward, that always seemed to simply embarrass him.

"We did meet the queen actually, at an RYA race in '82."

"That's what your wife said." The girl took a gulp of a breath, sloshing the ice in the jug against its sides. "You're kind of famous, right? I mean, you sailed around the world?"

"Not me. That sort of thing's for the elderly and people with too much time on their hands." He paused. Even he heard the snobbishness, a professional discussing things beneath him. Never mind that he and Top made a good deal of money from just those sorts of customers, the pretend blue-water types. "You're interested in sailing, then?"

"Sure, I mean, it's pretty. All those bright white boats out on a nice day. But I want to *go*. That's all I want. All over the world. Just get out there. Everywhere." She stood there looking down at him expectantly, waiting perhaps for him to ask about all the places she intended to go.

"Well, then," he said blandly. "The very best of luck to you."

She looked disappointed but smiled, a thin, uncertain smile that revealed a pointed canine crooking out of a row of closely packed teeth. Another man Lomax's age might have taken a casual, proprietary interest in the girl's future. But Lomax was of the opinion that people sorted out their own futures or, more generally, had it all sorted out for them. When she came with the check, it occurred that he might try to draw her out again. He tipped her thirty percent instead.

After that night, he only saw the girl on a couple of occasions, and on one of those she was sitting at the bar wrapping silverware. Then she disappeared altogether. On a blowy evening, nearly two months after Susan's funeral, he and Top were standing at the end of the main pier watching the last of the boats come in. It took a moment for Lomax to remember the girl's name—Jessica—from her name tag. He asked what had happened to her.

Top pushed up his sunglasses. There was a tricky cross-breeze. He squinted to watch a boat coming in and massaged the bridge of his nose between his thumb and forefinger, the same frustrated gesture he used to make when a cruiser he was skippering was running slow. Top had a long history with the club, took a hand in its operations, and didn't much like talking about it. Gossip traveled fast around the lake. Lomax thought he wasn't going to get an answer, but then Top said flatly, "Yeah, we had to let her go."

These things happen, Lomax thought. People came and went in those sorts of jobs. "She was always very charming with me."

"There were some complaints. Boundaries crossed."

For a reason he couldn't name, Lomax felt oddly dismayed by this small piece of news. Top dropped his sunglasses back onto his nose, turned to look out at the boat that was tacking in. It was a 24. Its spinnaker waggled hesitantly in front as the crew tried to make the dock. Lomax started to ask what kind of complaints, but just then Top called out to the boat.

"Christ, cut that thing in here!" A savage note came into Top's voice. "You're missing the whole damned pier. Bearing away! Jibe! Jibe!"

When Susan had been bedridden, she'd wanted certain of her possessions constantly in sight. A favorite scarf, a favorite sweater, the garden club tote bag she'd carried her books to school in. She'd moan or whimper if she didn't have them, and, over those last, long months, sometimes seemed more interested in those thread-worn things than in him. They were the first things he had boxed up and hidden away in the attic. He could hardly believe he so resented a tote bag.

He started the cleanup with some industry—throwing out the old sheets, her bath towels, her makeup—but his efforts quickly failed. He wandered from room to room, afraid to disturb anything, full of antic energy, yet too slothful to dust, vacuum, or even empty the dishwasher. Geralyn called every Sunday morning at eleven, waking him from dozing. It was five o'clock her time, and on the other end of the line he heard the clatter of saucepans as she got Sunday dinner ready, Norman in the background calling to their two teenage girls to set the table.

"Everyone's been very good at the shop," he said. "But I won't get anything done when they're all treating me like a poor widower."

"If you haven't felt like working," Geralyn said, "then enjoy yourself a little. You've given Top fifteen years already, haven't you? It's his company, not yours."

"I don't know what else I'd do. Work is work. My adventuring is behind me."

Geralyn breathed a sigh through the phone. Lomax knew she didn't have patience for tragic pronouncements. He wasn't fond of them either.

"Sell the house," she said. "Take a long holiday. You've got the means."

"Maybe I'll buy another boat. The *Elizabeth the Second*. The *Camilla Parker*."

She ignored his evasions. "Get a flat somewhere tropical. Shake yourself up a bit."

"I might sail around the world."

"Oh, Max, I don't want to nag. I'm worried about you. *Norman* is worried about you." She sighed again, but now her voice was tender, as if she were talking about the distant past. "But you always land on your feet, don't you? Infuriating for the rest of us, but you always do."

She meant to tease and reassure him, but he chose to hear her words as a complaint. "Please, Geri, have a little faith in me," he said. "I do have a life here."

"Well," she answered tartly, "get back to it then!"

That afternoon he swung the *Elizabeth* past Top's pier, hoping to catch Top and Linda at the lake. He slackened the sail and drifted, thinking they would come down any minute. The water was glassy, and he could see the white posts of the pier and the sugar maples on the near bank reflected, stretched out and gently quivering in the wavelets tipping their way toward shore. After a few minutes, Top and Linda's big white Akita came down the lawn, barked at him, then wandered back up to the house. Lomax dozed for a time, woke himself, waited another half hour, then brought the *Elizabeth* around and headed for the club.

He dropped anchor just inside the no-wake buoy, took off his shirt, and swam to the main pier. When he pulled himself up, he saw a young woman in sunglasses and a blue two-piece suit stretched out on a towel sunbathing. She gave him a casual, dismissive sort of wave. It took him a moment to recognize his waitress. "It's Lomax," he said, as if to remind her. Then he realized he'd never introduced himself at the restaurant.

She propped herself up on her elbows. "How'd you do that?" She pointed languidly at the top of his head. "Your sunglasses. You swam in, and they're still on."

He reached up and felt for them. "I didn't even notice. They're always up there."

"That's a tiny boat. I've seen twenty other boats go by, and they were all bigger."

"Where are your clothes?"

"In my car. Why?"

"Jessica," he said deliberately. He wanted to say it with as much understanding as he could. "This is a private pier."

"Who cares?" she said flatly. "I don't even want to swim."

"Listen, I'm not going to kick you off. But I'd look out for the manager if I were you."

She sat up and started peeling skin off her forearm. "It's Jake's day off."

"That's a nasty burn," he said. She was sweating a good deal, and he couldn't keep his eyes from lingering where it beaded the tops of her breasts and dampened the edges of her swimsuit. "Have you found more work?"

"I might start up with my mom. She cleans at a hotel. The big one at the golf resort."

"What does your father do?"

"He's at that hog farm out on County B."

He knew the farm, a local controversy. When the wind was to the east, the sour reek of the pens blew all the way to Kishwago. The thought that came next arrived all at once.

"Come clean for me," he said. "I don't have a regular person. I could use the help."

A moment of silence hung between them. God, what did he sound like? Maybe he did, in fact, want to be seen as the poor, noble widower. Even if he hadn't mentioned it, no doubt this girl knew Susan was gone.

"Okay," she said, "I'll find your address in the phone book." As if it had all been decided long before and she regularly provided this service for sad old men. She lay back out on the towel, adjusted her top. "I remember your name from your credit card."

At home Lomax sat on the patio with a Foster's. He took two gulps, put it down, and then forgot all about it. After a time, he got the Lexus out of the garage and drove into the country. On either side of the road, fields of mustard glowed with the light shining off the waxy leaves. He stopped at a gas station. Inside he waited until he was the only customer, walked up to the clerk, pointed to a rack of magazines behind the counter. "That one, top left." He didn't know the title and hardly cared. When he got back, he took it up to the bedroom, flipped through a few pages—felt Susan's presence all around him. He was so ashamed he threw the thing away.

11

Jessica came an hour late, a bucket full of cleaning supplies held in the crook of her arm. She wore jeans and a boy's Oxford with the sleeves rolled up. Lomax, in his shorts and sandals, was better dressed for the work. He'd already straightened up the bathroom and the kitchen in anticipation of her arrival.

"I'll start wherever you want." She put the bucket down in the middle of the kitchen. He watched her looking around the room—the marble counters, brushed-steel appliances, copper-clad cookware hanging from the pot rack, the photo on the fridge of Susan and him in dinner wear at the Auckland Yacht Club. "It's clean. You keep pretty clean for a guy."

"You have to keep everything in order onboard a cruiser. Couldn't move otherwise."

"Sure, but this is a pretty big house." She took the supplies out of her bucket, lined them up on the counter. All the bottles were still full to the top, just purchased. "Can I use your mop?"

"Have you done this before?"

She looked around again, for a place to begin. "Everyone knows how to clean."

"I thought you helped your mum." She smiled when he said "mum," but then her expression went blank again. "Only sometimes. That's why I had the job at your club." She sprayed the countertop, swiped at it with a rag from her bucket.

"I'm going off for a run," he said tentatively. "Let you work in peace."

"Have fun," she called over her shoulder. "Don't get a burn."

He went out in the heat of the day with a nearby park as his aim. A pain in his knee started nagging, but he ran through it. When he finally stopped for breath, his knee was throbbing. "Fine," he said to himself. "Fine."

He called out as he came through the door. No one answered. The air seemed charged, as if he were entering a stranger's house. The mop was propped against the fridge door, a smear of soapy water dragged after it. He found the girl sitting on the couch in the living room, head in hands. Before he could ask what was wrong, she pointed to the corner, where a small vase lay on the carpet, broken into three neat pieces.

"Another thing I fucked up," Jessica said and then burst into tears.

At the sound of her crying, panic thundered over him, and for a moment he couldn't speak or even move. Then, underneath the panic, something else came welling up, a giddy feeling almost like joy, and he wanted to laugh or cry out. He fought to calm himself, to keep his voice from shaking. "It's all right," he said, crouching to pick up the pieces of the vase, his knee making him wince. "Never mind."

They met eyes for a moment. "Was it hers?"

"Just a trinket. I think we bought it in the night market in Baguio."

Her tears heaved up into sobs.

"Come on," he said. "Come outside, get a breath of air."

They went down to the shore path. There was chop on the lake, only a handful of boats on the water. They walked along the path without meeting anyone. It was midweek, thank god, and most of his neighbors were away. A quarter mile from Top and Linda's house on Black Point, Lomax stopped to turn back around.

"I want to replace it," Jessica said, rubbing her red eyes with the heels of her palms. "You don't have to pay me."

"Don't be silly," he murmured.

She stood looking at the opposite shore, toward the three white piers and the anchor. "Nobody owns a stupid lake," she said.

"Well, it is a club." He didn't know what else to say. "Suppose I would've been the same at your age." Though it had always been Susan who felt tentative around the yachting crowd.

He led them back along the path. The wind was whipping up. The rushing of the maples lining the shore seemed to be everywhere. A sharp, metallic taste burred the back of his throat. Nerves, perhaps, but he felt strangely light and clearheaded.

"Are you off to school come autumn?" he said. "University perhaps?"

She clenched her jaw, didn't answer.

"Well, I didn't go in for academics either. I was a jock."

"I want to go all these places. I have these guidebooks. I look at them all the time." She spoke hurriedly, her breath catching. "All my brothers and cousins ever want to do is work on their cars and hang out in the Burger King parking lot."

"Well, don't worry. It's the same boring people all over the world." He laughed, as if including himself in that category.

She looked at him skeptically, hungrily. "Tell me about one of the places you've been."

"Well, we . . ." He was saved by the chugging of a jet ski. The craft and rider, thumping across the waves, came into view. "Christ," Lomax said, "I'll have that racket all afternoon."

"Must be tough." The little, pointed tooth reappeared.

Lomax laughed again, a gentle, unrestrained laugh that surprised him, it sounded so unfamiliar. The girl stopped and looked back toward Black Point, where the whitecaps converged and the surface of the lake frothed to a clean, powder white. She stood there, held by the view, as if it were the most striking thing. Lomax couldn't help picturing her inside a small, dark house, like the ones he'd seen on the outskirts of Delevan—the television flashing in the corner, something frying noisily in the kitchen, a baby crying, her father stomping in at night, reeking of the hog pens. He wondered what a girl like her hoped for. Stable, pleasant work, some young romance, maybe in a few years a baby she could show off to friends. By the time he and Susan had finally stopped their globe-trotting and settled in Kishwago, they'd both felt too old for children. Susan put her energy into her teaching. Neither of them was the sort to complain or talk about their regrets, and if one of them was left here alone now, well, they'd always known it could happen. It didn't help anything to talk about regrets.

Jessica rubbed her eyes again, kneading the last tears from them. When she looked at him again, her eyes shone with a vitality it almost pained him to see. "Well, better get a move on," he said and started back toward the house. She lingered another moment.

"Jesus, it's beautiful here!" she shouted out across the water, as if she was calling out to make an echo. And to his surprise, one came faintly back. ". . . beautiful here . . . beautiful . . ."

He didn't expect her to return, but she came again, the next several weeks, with her bucket of supplies and her boy's shirt. He let her pick her away around the house, staying out of her way, working upstairs while she cleaned downstairs. He heard her whistling or singing the words to pop songs he didn't recognize, then the sound of chairs being shifted around, the creaking of the mechanism that wrung out the mop, the television's chatter. It was strange to have the silence of the house pierced so casually. He came down one afternoon to find she'd rearranged half the furniture in the living room. "It's more open this way," she explained. In the other sitting room, she straightened and organized Susan's bookshelves. She offered to iron his shirts, said she liked ironing. But she left creases. He spent an hour redoing them after she'd driven away in her red hail-pocked Nissan Sentra.

The shop floor manager called one morning about a difficult order. Lomax hesitated a few days before contacting the customer, a nervy young guy in San Francisco who'd made his money in software and thought his technical mind meant he understood boat physics. "No, of course, we can recut the hull," Lomax said patiently. "Wouldn't recommend it, but, yes, it can be done." The customer told him he'd checked with the competition. They would've done the boat he wanted for sixty grand less, and they wouldn't have bitched about it, either. Lomax felt his cheeks going hot.

"Why don't we meet halfway?" he heard himself saying. "We'd like to keep your business." And then he suggested a truly absurd discount. He couldn't stand to see any boat, even a complete disaster, get scrapped.

For the rest of the day, he stalked around the house muttering to himself. But it had felt good too. It felt good to talk about boats, even with a goddamn desk jockey nub who didn't know a thing about them.

He'd given Jessica a front door key. He called down when he heard her letting herself in—"Don't mind me! Just up here getting a few things done"—and resumed his anxious pacing. He'd started on Susan's closets again, stuffing black bin bags full of clothes, piling up the hangers on the bed, making a separate heap of things he'd indiscriminately decided to keep. After an hour, he felt his body thrumming, exhaustion or excitement, he didn't know which. He went down and put on the tea, interrupting Jessica in her cleaning, chattering to her in a voice that sounded curiously high-pitched in his own ears, about the weather, the drought they were supposed to get, and how many miles and what pace he'd done on his exercise bike that morning.

"No clue if that's good or bad," she teased him. "But sure sounds impressive."

"I'm trying to impress you, am I?"

"The guys in my school always talked about how much they could bench."

"Ah, the life of the jock! Numbers, always numbers."

Jessica leaned against the counter. She wore a red tank top and gray sweat shorts with the name of her high school across the thigh. It was late summer now, and she was very tanned. Her complexion had cleared up considerably, and she'd let her hair grow long. She crossed one leg over the other at the ankle and stretched her back against the counter, grinning at him.

"You're the boss at your company, right?"

"More of a glorified salesman," he said.

"I bet you're persuasive."

"Only one rule in sailing—the guy with the most expensive boat wins."

“Sounds like a fun sport.”

“They haven’t ruined it completely.” He laughed. “Not yet anyway.”

He went back up to Susan’s things, feeling strange, like he was vibrating. Jessica called up that she was finished. “Next week, then!” he called back. He heard the Sentra moving up the driveway as he sat on the edge of the bed staring at the black bags—fifteen of them—resolved to take them to the Salvation Army and just get rid of them. But that night they only found their way from the bedroom to the attic.

The following weeks, they developed a routine. Jessica brought a little speaker with her, and as she worked, she turned the volume up loud on her hyperactive pop music. He’d make her a turkey sandwich and a cup of tea, and she’d eat at the kitchen table, flipping through a fashion magazine Susan had subscribed to and that kept coming even after he canceled it. Once, taking a break, Jessica had stretched out on one of the patio chairs. From the upstairs window, he could see her in her blue bikini and shorts, the magazine steepled over her lap. When he looked next, she’d put on Susan’s old, wide-brimmed straw hat. For a moment, he thought it was his wife, and his heart leaped up, not with joy but terror that he could be so easily mistaken.

Sometimes he’d eat lunch with her. “The expert’s guide to luscious lips,” Jessica read aloud to him. “At thirty-five, she changed her life by switching to soy.” She giggled. “Sixteen top secrets for driving him wild.” She licked the crumbs off her lips as she skimmed the articles. “My friend John said I should be a model. Ha, right. My teeth are way too messed up. But I don’t know, maybe I’ll go to beauty school. Take out a loan, learn to cut some fancy hair.”

“That sounds a sensible idea,” he said, measuring his words carefully. Hearing her speak so idly about her future plans made him somehow heartsick.

“What, don’t think I can do it? Or is cutting hair too trashy?”

He hesitated before answering. “I think at your age you can do anything.”

"Jeez, thanks!" she said, rolling her eyes. "Some advice." She put down the magazine. "Was your wife always a teacher?"

His reply came reluctantly. "She waitressed for a time, though mostly we lived on the cheap, waited for the next race, traveled a little in between."

"You guys were lucky."

"Yes, we had some good fortune," he said softly. "A long stretch of it, anyway."

"I'm sorry, didn't mean to . . ." Her face went flush. "She was young for a stroke, right?"

"Some people are just susceptible. That's all the doctors could say in the end."

"What was it like when she was sick?"

"It was quiet. Sometimes it was hard to believe she was still shut up in there, in her body . . . All very quiet," he said again.

For the rest of the day, he found himself quietly repeating Jessica's words. *You were lucky*. What had Susan said to him all those years ago? "Very lucky me." But Susan was the one person who'd never made any demands on luck, whose personality was too great and generous to require it. He pictured the hog farm, the dark little house on the outskirts of Delevan. And then he thought of Ditchling and the rather ordinary semidetached he and Geralyn had grown up in. Yes, he'd been lucky. His career had taken him around the world. But he had never steered. He'd left that to Susan. The whole time he'd just been following in her wake.

On the phone with Geralyn that Sunday, he was unusually talkative, asking questions about Norman and the girls. A card had come in the mail from Top and Linda, he told his sister. Top was celebrating his sixtieth birthday the weekend before Labor Day.

"Yes, I know about that," Geralyn said. "Linda wrote me. She writes every other week. I think she misses Susan, and I'm the surrogate."

"I never noticed you two making friends."

"Well, you wouldn't, would you?"

What he didn't mention was the note Top had scrawled on the back of the invitation. *Haven't seen much of you, Max. But here's my big day. Got to drag you out for a night at least.* And then, below that, even more hastily scribbled, *Really need to see you, buddy.* He could almost picture Top massaging the bridge of his nose as he wrote it.

"Perhaps you'll meet someone at the party," Geralyn said.

"Geri, it's a little soon, isn't it." In that typically English way, his questions were statements, his statements, questions. "Besides, I'm not interested in meeting anyone."

"Stretching out the grief isn't heroic, Max. Put yourself out there a little. Susan was larger than life. She drowned you out a little."

He didn't protest. It was true, and it was exactly what he had loved about her.

The following week, he came downstairs with some costume jewelry he thought Jessica might like. Better that than throw it away. He called her name. She didn't respond. He found her sitting at the dining table. In front of her was a photo album. She had it open to the middle, a page of photos of Susan and him sitting on a white sand beach with banana plants in the background.

"I remember her voice from school," Jessica said, pointing to a photo in which Susan was especially beautiful. "Weird how pictures make everything come back. Hearing that voice took me, like, a million miles away." He stood looking over her shoulder while she paged through the album. Susan in front of a waterfall, her chestnut hair frizzy with mist—Bali. Susan in a party frock, mouth wide open, laughing, bottle of champagne dangling from her hand—Port-au-Prince.

A smile spread across Jessica's face, her thin lips just covering the tooth. "It's like another planet. No corn or anything."

"It can be beautiful here too," he said, almost whispering. "When the mustard fields glow in the sun . . . Ordinary beauty. You learn to appreciate it."

"Sure. Hog stink and everything."

He didn't know whether to laugh. He felt the closeness, the warmth of her body. He pointed to a photo of Susan and him posing on a hotel terrace, an amber sunset and desert as backdrop. "That's Al Jubayl. Closed to Westerners. They wanted the team to sail an exhibition."

Jessica's finger followed his, brushing against it. "And this one?"

He looked down at their two fingers lying on the page, pointing to yet another picture of Susan when she was young and beautiful and strong.

He pushed the album away suddenly and moved into the living room. Jessica rose from the table to follow, and before he could say anything, she had her arms around him, her head on his chest. She took his hand, clumsily interlacing their fingers. "Don't worry." The words sounded dully in him like the muffled blows of a hammer. "It's okay."

"Jessica, I don't want you to misinterpret—"

She pressed closer, and he felt himself straining toward her. Under his khaki trousers, he was growing erect. He closed his eyes, trying to force those images of Susan from his thoughts. *She'd made herself sick.* Yes, she'd done it to spite him—for taking her from her home, her family, for everything his itinerant life had denied them.

In truth, neither of them had been too old for children by the time they arrived here. No, he'd felt too *young*, too reluctant to give up on past glories. "Athletes never retire," he'd once told Susan, "they just give up." He'd meant it as a joke, but they both heard that he wouldn't let a child moor him to any single port, that their life together had always been pursuing his glories, not Susan's. And he felt that, however little she'd dwelled in hurt, she'd never forgiven him—that, after her stroke, she no longer concealed her true feelings. The way she always turned away from him . . . She'd lain there in that bed all those long months, shut inside herself, just to spite him. He saw her again, her head turned into the pillow, a tear sliding down her cheek. Oh, for fuck's sake, why not? Why couldn't he just take what this girl was offering?

"You don't have to worry," Jessica said again. "I'm old enough. I want to help."

"Jessica," he said, "please." His voice shook. His palms were sweating. He abruptly took his hand from hers, separated the two of them. She stood almost perfectly still, staring at the carpet. "Jessica, I really . . . Listen, if we weren't so differ— No, you should go home now."

"I still have to vacuum."

"That's enough for today."

"It's what you pay me for, isn't it?"

"I can finish the rest. I can manage."

He found his checkbook in the kitchen and wrote out a check. He heard her gathering her things and dropping them in her bucket. As they moved around each other, he felt himself trembling. It was all he could do to keep from pulling her to him again.

He walked her out to her car. It was a clear, bright day, and a hard, flat glare came off every surface. They stood before her hail-pocked Nissan, the divots in the hood making little pools of light. Jessica looked up at him. Her expression darkened. "I didn't want it to go that way. It's just that I wanted to ask you . . ."

"What is it, Jessica?"

"I want to go back to your club. As your guest."

He smiled thinly, shook his head. "Don't be silly, now."

"There's no law against it."

"Jessica, please."

"You let me into your house." Something flashed behind her eyes. "Yes, I know what you really pay me for."

"This place would be a tip without you." He faltered, tried to summon up his charm. "An utter tip. You're a great help. But I can't—"

She hauled up her bucket, opened the trunk, and dropped it in with a clatter. "Shit," she said, looking away. "It's just a job, right? Another shitty job. This house creeps me out anyway."

"You've been terribly good, Jessica. I really don't think I could manage without—"

"No, I get it. The help is just supposed to disappear." She got into her car, fumbled for a moment pulling the foil sun reflector off the dash. "Didn't want to confuse things for you."

"Jessica," he said. "Jessica—"

She looked up at him then, so injured and questioning he couldn't say any more. "You all think you're the center of the fucking world."

"Jessica, please don't—"

She chunked the car into gear, lurched up the drive, tires spitting gravel, and went out of sight in the trees. Her brakes whined as she braked at the top of the drive to turn onto the road, and then the car stalled out. He heard her turn it over once, then twice before it caught again. And then she was gone, and he heard nothing but the wind in the treetops.

That Sunday, Geralyn's call woke him early. "Sorry, Max," she piped into the phone. "We're off to the cinema for the afternoon. Have you seen it on the news? The summit? 'Yo, Blair.' Makes you ashamed doesn't it?" She was trying to get in enough small talk that their conversation wouldn't feel rushed. Even these calls—his other lifeline to the world—had become routine.

"Really, Geri, have you ever heard me give a damn about politics?"

"What's gotten into you?"

"Don't bother checking in on me all the time. Bully your own family for a change."

He heard scuffling on the other end of the line, the kettle whistling, the dying note as it came off the burner. He made a feeble attempt to apologize, but Geralyn cut him short. "I don't know what you're on about, Max, but we've a nice day out planned, and I won't have you ruining it. You might have gone half round the world, but you've never really left home, have you?" And then she hung up before he could ask just what that meant.

The following Tuesday, though he wanted to see Jessica and explain again, he left a note saying he was out on the dining room table along with a check. He figured she wouldn't even show up, but when he came back late that afternoon, the kitchen floor was still wet, the mop left out, footprints on the tile, the job finished but only half done. He took up the mop himself, but after a few minutes, the air in the house felt so close he couldn't breathe. He went outside, following the shore path, staring blankly out at the late afternoon sun quivering on the limpid water. Supposed to be healed by now, he kept thinking. Supposed to be moving ahead. Luck had pulled him through his life, and now it had stranded him here in these horse latitudes. For a week, he hardly left the house. He kept the curtains drawn, the phone off the hook.

He left another note for Jessica. Perhaps it was better for both of them, it read, if they put the job on hiatus. He wished her good luck with future endeavors. He put the note in a little beige envelope he found in Susan's bureau, left it on the counter with another check, this one for a hundred over the usual amount, and then went out clothes shopping. He'd lost even more weight recently. He wandered the aisles of the local department store, feeling the sleeves of the sport coats, wondering how it even mattered what he wore to Top's party. When he got back that evening, the high smell of bleach hung in the air. The house had been cleaned immaculately. In a state near to panic, he dug through the scraps of paper he kept by the phone. Jessica had written down a number where he could reach her. He'd never used it. Why couldn't he help her? He could give her the loan she'd talked about. She could go to beauty school, get her teeth fixed. He could give her some advice. He could give her that, at least. What sounded like a teenage boy answered on the fifth ring.

"Who's this?" the voice said. "Where you calling from, man?"

It was Lomax, calling for Jessica.

"Oh, you're that English guy. The guy with the boat, wining and dining my sister."

No, no, Lomax said. There was some kind of misunderstanding. Jessica worked for him. Was she in? He needed to talk to her.

"Shit, dude," the teenage voice said, "how old is you, anyway?

III

The club was lit up for the party. A huge cluster of balloons tied to the front awning dipped and spun in the breeze. In the entryway, there was a photo spread of Top at various stages of his career. Lubber, nub, crew, cup competitor, captain . . . Lomax stood scrutinizing it all, listening to the voices and laughter, wanting very badly to turn around and go home.

There were seventy or eighty people in the banquet hall. A whole room of people who were going to reminisce about Susan, ask how he was, how he was holding up. Or maybe, nearly half a year later, it was too late for all of that. Somehow that seemed worse. His grief, his desperation—already old news. He found Linda standing with a small circle of women and said his hellos. He felt their eyes on him, heard himself responding to Linda, and a moment later forgot what he'd said. He excused himself, stepped out onto the terrace, and stood under the floodlight in a cloud of gnats, hand cupped over his mouth, forcing himself to take deep breaths.

Someone came up the lawn, a shadow detaching itself from the other shadows. He wore a pressed shirt with a fleece vest over it, a sun-bleached ball cap. He paused on the threshold between the darkness and the floodlit terrace. Behind him, the anchor stood in silhouette against the gray sky and the dark water. "Hiding out like me?"

"Happy birthday," Lomax said to his old skipper.

Top came onto the terrace and leaned against the stucco wall. "Been turning old for a long time, but here it is." The two of them stood there with the insects darting around them. The lake was there, the sloshing of the waves, the dark outline of the anchor against the shifting, crawling dark. "Chicago show last week. Some nice boats down there. Stiff competition."

"Every year." Sound carried strangely near water. Murmuring voices came across the lake, the cracking hiss of beer cans being opened. "Got a speech ready?"

"Short and sappy," Top said. "Get it over with. Get back to life."

"I'm trying to remember what that's like."

Top reached in his pocket, took out a pack of cigarettes. "Cheer up, buddy. Late in the race, but we can still pull it out." He exhaled the smoke from his nostrils. The gnats swam away, gathered again. "Give me my swan song, Max, but I'm on the way out. There's the whole operation to run if you want it."

"Of course."

"You can tell me no for once in your life."

Lomax's stomach felt leaden. He'd always thought this would be a happy moment. He'd always dreamed of bringing the news home to Susan. "I'm telling you yes."

"Thank you, sailor. Means the world." Top knelt, carefully ground the cigarette out on the terrace, dropped it into a potted plant, turned to go inside. "Let's go face the firing squad."

"Skip," Lomax said, "I wanted to ask you . . ."

Top gave him a questioning, impatient look. It was settled. That was how Top worked. Yes or no. There wasn't anything else to discuss.

"That girl fired from the restaurant. What were the complaints?" Nothing changed in Top's expression. "Petite girl," Lomax went on. "Pretty. Jessica, I think her name was."

"Oh, her. She was begging rides from members, hanging out on the pier all day, some kind of pick-up act, gold digging probably. Our members want to be comfortable, Max."

"Right," he said weakly. "Always."

When they went inside, someone put a Foster's in his hand. Lomax moved from conversation to conversation, talking mostly about Top, telling the same handful of stories to each group, on autopilot, sometimes breaking off in the middle to get another beer.

He found himself talking to a woman he didn't know, a friend of someone or other, staying in their guesthouse for the weekend. She lived and worked in the Loop, came to Kishwago whenever she could. So picturesque, the lake, such a quaint little town. Yes, of course, Lomax said. Center of the world. The woman laughed, though he hadn't said anything funny. She was somewhere in her forties and wore a good deal of carefully applied makeup. She talked quickly, saying repeatedly how bored she was at the party.

At some point in the night, there was a toast to Top, a series of boozy speeches. Lomax watched his friend standing stiffly at the front of the room, listening to all the fond jokes, praise, and accolades, smiling and nodding uncertainly as if he had heard of the man worthy of this event without having met him. At some point, Lomax and the woman slipped out. The drive was only a smear across his memory. At his front door, he fumbled with his keys while she stood giggling at him. A moment later, he had her pressed up against the kitchen counter, her sundress up over her waist. "No, no"—she shook her head dramatically, her blond hair, brown at the roots, falling over her eyes—"take me to bed already."

He sat on the edge of the mattress, reeling. She pulled him to her, kissed him roughly, but he pushed her away. "What? What's wrong?" She put her arms around him again. Then the weight of desire was too much, and he went ahead in a dull frenzy, until his hip bones ached.

He woke in the night, still drunk. The smell of sweat and sex filled the room, and for a moment he couldn't help luxuriating in the idea that he might wake this woman snoring in his bed and do it all over again. Then the memory of another night slid forward.

It had been early in the process—the doctors had called it that, a "process"—when there was still an outside chance Susan might recover.

That night, when he touched her like he'd been used to, she didn't understand what was happening. What had he thought, that he could somehow coax her back to herself, salvage them both? She struck out at him feebly, hitting him in the chest, the face. He had to grip her by the shoulders, hold her still. Afterward, he lay there in the dark beside her. Finally, he'd gone into the bathroom, found a face towel, used it to dry her tears.

Now he pulled on his T-shirt and shorts, went down the hallway. It took him three attempts, but finally he got hold of the ring to the attic hatch, yanked down the collapsible ladder.

At the lake, he stuffed the sweater and scarf into the tote bag, then went out onto the pier and started to unmoor the *Elizabeth*. When he stepped into the boat, the drink and the motion of the waves nearly toppled him. He righted himself again and pushed off, then worked methodically, brute muscle memory, putting up the sail. When the wind caught it, he felt a sudden hollowness in his chest, as if he were folding in on himself. He looked toward the middle of the lake—the black void swaying before him—took the tiller in hand and set his course.

FLIGHT OF THE DODO

At the bottom of the crater, distances were absurd. The shadows were so long and dark they seemed part of the topography. Cady had to keep telling herself those weren't canyons before her. The sun was at her back, and as she put the tended area of the crater farther behind her, the shadows broadened, climbed into a glacier of darkness. Ahead, maybe two hundred yards, she thought she saw a patch of dark gray tracing high arcs, flinging up faint, shimmering clouds of dust. Her senses were so wide open, she couldn't be sure. Her blood was roaring in her ears. The smell of him lingered in her suit, so close, so present she felt she could reach out and touch him.

When Cady floated into Kumar's private cabin, she found him still strapped in, his eyes closed, arms squeezed tight against his sides. The other Luminaries had all sat in observation for the launch, started the party together, but Kumar had taken the big ride on his own.

"Hey, there!" Cady said, sounding to herself like a goddamn restaurant hostess. "Felt like someone dropped a piano on you, right? You keep everything down? Training don't do it justice. Salmon croquettes from last night come sailing right back up."

Kumar slowly opened his eyes, a prolonged wince uncoupling. Maybe the launch had panicked him—being hurled aloft and hammered down all at once—but he met her gaze with unnerving calm. "Well, yes," he said, "quite the jolt."

She knew his dossier: Mother was Spanish, the Duquesa of something or other. Father ran India's biggest telecom. And Kumar, the younger, had spent his childhood in British schools and the rest of his thirty-seven years jetting around the marble for the family charity. He was the youngest of the Luminaries and had passed all the fitness tests, trumped up as they were, with an air of wry distraction. The day before the flight, he'd had his wavy crest of hair shorn down to stubble. The Nu-Luna uniform (*a lustrous aubergine*, the promotional copy read, *accented by an underlayer of proprietary woven alloy*) showed off the hard lines of his body. Cady had to tell herself not to stare.

"Now, if you look starboard, to your right," she added, back in hostess mode, "you'll see the curve of the thermosphere." Over Argentina, the sun was rising, a band of orange bleeding into a band of dark blue, then dark purple, the upper atmosphere a pale halo above that. "Now, don't tell me you didn't even peek the whole way up."

A shine flickered into Kumar's eyes as he regarded the view. "Unparalleled," he said. "Magnificent, truly." Lord, that accent, so elegant, so deflating.

She helped him undo his straps. He floated up, pushed off the ceiling, took an experimental trip across the cabin. Cady felt her own body unmangling from lift-off. Nothing unusual, except, watching him, her stomach kept hopping around like it was her first time up.

"What fun," he said. "Much better than the training."

"Yessir, we ain't in the vomit comet no more!" She'd cultivated an east-Texas drawl over the years, always thought she'd be known by it. Down-home just sounded right getting beamed back to Mission Control. "We're having us a little celebration in observation. Come on up, join in!"

Kumar shot across the cabin, and she put out a hand to slow him. They drifted against his bunk, where he floated just above her lap. She swallowed hard—typical zero-G congestion, she told herself—gave him a little shove that sent him into a slow twist. He caught himself on the opposite wall, and she admired again his compact physique, the grooves of his well-developed forearms, her favorite part of a man's body. Despite herself, she thought of Kip. And then she thought of a blank, a void, a vacuum.

Kumar didn't answer about going up to observation. He was probably used to not having to answer the help. "Something to sharpen the appetite then." Cady reached behind the bulkhead, where she'd stashed a bottle of champagne on the way in. From the pocket of her uniform, she took a small nylon bladder and a zip strip. She strapped the bladder to the bottle, pushed her thumbs in under the cork. It popped with a hollow thud. She quickly cinched the bladder with the strip, pulled it off the bottle, pierced it with a narrow metal tube and, holding it up to demonstrate, opened the valve and sent a stream of champagne into her mouth.

"When Napoleon's soldiers won in battle, they used to take their sabers, slice the tops right off the bottles, drink the champagne in about three gulps. We're a little more restrained up here." She gave the bladder a push and sent it sputniking over to him. "I'm a bit of a history buff. What they call 'well-rounded.'" You had to have a little banter prepared, they'd told her at Johnson, for the folks down below.

Kumar took a taste. "*Blanc de Noirs*. Thoughtful choice."

Holding the bladder under his arm like a set of bagpipes, he sent a pale, golden stream quivering in her direction. She moved toward it, opened her mouth, let it slide right to the back of her throat, bubbles fizzling all the way down. "Look at you," she said, "already an ace." He sent another sliver her way. She made a show of slurping it up with a slow in-suck of her cheeks. "Hmmm. Just tastes better up here."

"Your method aerates it. Brings out the finish."

"Well, us space jocks learn to improvise." She let a sultry smile cross her face. "Never know what might happen."

Unofficially, the company encouraged them to carouse and even flirt with the Luminaries. *Drab has been done*, their leonine, perma-tanned CEO had purred in Nu-Luna's first big press conference, while a model slinked around the stage in a formfitting prototype of the uniform. *Let's give superorbital flight some curves.*

"How's about we check out this shindig up front?" Cady said again.

Kumar was turning solemn pirouettes and corkscrews. He came slowly to rest as an image fluttered onto the screen at the foot of his bunk: the live feed from the crater, the view stark, digitally precise, eerily still.

He put his hand to his stomach, seeming unable to pull his gaze from the screen. "I'm still a bit unsettled, I'm afraid. My apologies." Out of the starboard window, the gauzy aura of the outer atmosphere dissolved into fathomless black space. "I very much hate to be an inconvenience."

It was Cady's sixth time up. Add to that seven hundred plus hours in the training sim, and she knew every readout, valve, and handhold on both decks of *Big Ambition*. Better maybe than she knew her half-empty house back down in Houston. Yet the ship still felt unfamiliar, its flowing, eggplant-hued contours aiming for soothing but coming off as weirdly dildo-like. Exiting Kumar's cabin, she pulled herself down the gangway, past the galley and crew cabin, pausing to check the pressure, temperature, and liquid oxygen readouts, a few minutes of solitude in the belly of Big A's muted humming and clicking. Then she opened the hatch separating the back half of the ship from the front, sounding a buzzer, and pulled herself into observation. Everyone turned to look, their bodies drifting into alphabetic positions of anticipation.

She had to keep from busting out laughing. They all wore the same purple uniform—red trim for crew, platinum for the Luminaries—and together in one room, they looked like some kind of space-age drill team, zipped up and glistening like a bruise. She arranged her features into solemnity but couldn't help an eye roll. Benjamin, the hospitality officer, gave her an aggrieved look and went back to serving postlaunch hors d'oeuvres.

There were four Luminaries besides Kumar. The jolly, brutal-looking man with the tips of his droopy mustache wagging above his lips was the Uzbek Interior minister, who'd probably paid his fare in gold and uranium nuggets. He resumed his study of the view from one of the panorama windows: an expanse of cloud-feathered ocean edged by the scrawl of Africa's coastline. At the other window, the two tech billionaires were deep in conversation over pouches of Bud Light Altitude. She could never keep their names straight. Right from first rounds of capitalization, Nu-Luna had been besieged by techheads and new-space fanboys. These two wore special patches with their corporate logos surrounded by twinkling stars and were planning to carry out experiments of their own design on the surface—all very cute. Finally, there was the Chinese babe, trophy wife of some ex-party official. Media attention had trailed off after Nu-Luna's first couple of flights, but this at least had made the news: The chick had an inoperable something or other and was spending the last of the dynasty's fortune on her dream.

Cady propelled herself over to Benjamin, who was serving up a rehydrated *brie en croûte*. "Cady, *there* you are." He swiveled around at the hips, peering this way and that, as if he were missing something. "And Mr. Kumar isn't well?"

Of course. They'd all been waiting for Kumar. During the Luminaries' training at the Celestuary, Kumar's easy, charity-event manners had seemed like the only thing pulling this group together. Six times up. For all of the company's early, vaulting talk about *the surging dynamism of private enterprise* and *man's eternal desire to reach higher, higher*, it already felt like they were just some ultra-exclusive ferry service—marble to the rock, rock to the marble. But Kumar had somehow imparted a handsome dignity to all of the over-rehearsed mission prep, a skill honed over a hundred fundraisers, no doubt, a way of showing everyone around him, with just the luster in his eyes, that, yes, all of this was necessary, vital, noble even.

"Kumar?" Cady said. "Shoot, he's fine. Just taking a little breather."

"Oh, no," the Chinese babe said, drifting over. "Mr. Kumar misses all the fun."

"And how are you feeling, Mrs. Hu? Liftoff kicks like a mule, don't it?"

"But I am sustained by the great beauty of space." Mrs. Hu wilted, took on a poignant expression. "I would hate to miss even one moment."

Cady laid a hand on the woman's withered, chicken-bone arm. "I think you're just so brave."

"When I finally see it, I think everything will be okay."

"It's magnificent," Cady said. "It really is. Unparalleled."

Cady and Benjamin floated to the side to confer.

"They're not complaining yet, are they?"

"It seems Mr. Kumar can be quite the brooder," Benjamin said. "Oops, come here, friend." He plucked an errant particle of brie from the air, popped it in his mouth. "Anyway, get him up here. You know how Captain McPhee feels about all the Luminary team building stuff."

"Look, they can't complain about Mr. Kumar not participating."

"I know *you're* not complaining," Benjamin said. "Got him all to yourself."

"Oh, please."

Had she betrayed some real, unstaged attraction during training or preflight? She'd met her husband, Kip, fifteen years ago, when she was at CalTech and he was doing X-jet test flights out of Edwards, chasing the smell of kerosene and ozone. They'd both been gunning for the Johnson Center, got their postings within a week of each other, bought the house in Houston three months after that, a poster couple, trotted out every time the Agency went after Minerva funding, the next phase, the new hope, the moonshot and beyond.

"I know, I know"—Benjamin clasped her shoulder—"you're the flight officer. Too much on your mind. Why don't *I* peek in on Mr. Kumar?"

"Ah, fuck you."

The two tech billionaires turned to look. Benjamin gave them an enormous smile, but they were just signaling for another round of drink pouches.

"That's all right, Ben," Cady said. "You're plenty busy."

When she glanced behind her, Little Ambition, the landing module, was already out of sight. In her wake, plumes of dust were rising in slow motion, each tiny particle throwing out its comet tail of shadow. It was raining shadows. She headed up the slope of the crater, each bound covering fifteen, twenty feet. She drifted over a crevice like a spill of ink, and a shiver went through her. Hundreds of feet down—you could disappear that quick—reason enough not to let the Luminaries wander. "Good boy, good boy," she'd joked when Kumar, almost shyly, had asked if he might step off the marked-out path. "Sure, you can go off leash. Just a little while." She'd attended to the minister for a moment, and when she turned back . . .

Another buzzer sounded as she let herself into the pilots' cabin.

"Well, look at this, Jimson," McPhee said, glancing back. "A rare sighting: the last of the Dodos." McPhee cinched himself tighter in the captain's chair and turned back to regard the black velvet depths of space. "Forgive me, Ms. Cady. Having a little fun on ya." He blinked several times, like a man woken from heavy sleep. "How's things back there? Everyone floating around, giggling like school kids?"

Next to him, Jimson—the copilot, who, like Benjamin, had come right out of Nu-Luna's own "academy"—was flipping and flipping through the goddamn safety test switches, something he'd done at least ten times since launch, trying to make himself look important.

"Pressure looks good," Cady said. "L-Ox right where it should be."

Jimson paused in his flipping. "Wonderful. And how are our guests?"

On the first couple of flights, their condescension—treating her like a glorified stewardess—was tongue-in-cheek. Now they didn't even bother to dress it up.

"Oh, they're hobnobbing away. You boys been playing your video games?"

Neither of them answered. Captain and copilot were mostly around for the landing. The trip was almost all flown by wire; McPhee and Jimson might as well have been on the sim for all they mattered up here. Never mind that back at Johnson, Cady had outscored every other astronaut candidate on the trainer. She'd even beat out Kip. He'd let her tease him about it. In their AsCan class, they were the shining stars, the burning bright comets, center of all of the drunken carousing at the Outpost. Kip had been so beautiful. Hours spinning in the Aerotrim, his twentieth suited dunk in the water survival tank—he still came out grinning. Hell, half of the Minerva program seemed built on that grin, on the two of them going up together, the idols of every schoolboy and -girl in the country.

"Shoot, what else you fellas got to do *but* play your games?" She gave the back of Jimson's chair a bump. "This bus practically drives itself."

Jimson turned and glared at her now. McPhee took it in stride.

"Well, shucks," McPhee said, stroking one of the instrument panels, which flashed a color-coordinated purple. "She was a mite temperamental back in October."

Along with their CEO, McPhee was one of the faces of Nu-Luna—late-middle-aged, senatorial, like he should be mugging on a box of hair dye—just the right amount of swashbuckling and fatherly for their cargo of interplanetary rubberneckers. McPhee had been smart. He'd gotten in ground-floor, flying joyride orbiters for Saudi royal family outings and Silicon Valley bachelor parties. Probably hated every second. But he'd seen what was coming.

"What's for lunch, Cady?" Jimson said.

"Why don't you head on back, find out?"

"Getting pretty famished. Burned up all that adrenalin on launch. Wouldn't say no to a little special delivery."

"You're a full-time thrill jockey, Jimson. I've always said that."

"What do ya reckon, Ms. Cady?" McPhee was from West Virginia, Yeager country. He was the only one in the company who out-drawled her. "Fudge swirl, caramel pecan, mint chocolate, or Snickers crunch? Missus won't let me have any of 'em back on the marble."

She didn't give a shit what ice cream McPhee had and nearly said as much. But just then Big Ambition made a course correction, a sound like a colt snorting, and into view swung the moon. It wasn't much larger than it was from the ground—still three hundred thousand klicks to go—but she was always unprepared: the way it cast its silvery light, its cryptic soliloquy. Strange, the thing that stood for distance and loneliness and endless walks in the park by her big, empty house, Kip's wings in her pocket—to have it, once more, assert its might.

"Jesus . . ." Jimson began. McPhee flinched and started blinking like a mole again. Cady just smiled, as if to welcome an old friend.

Every class that graduated Johnson got a nickname. Her class: "the Dodos." They'd never fly. It wasn't one thing but a hundred: another eastern European entanglement, dengue rioting across Florida and Georgia, the Potomac breaching its levees, the American taxpayer in full revolt. The Agency never said, officially, that it was mothballing Minerva. She and Kip had held on to hope; they'd climb right back into their lives, once things on the marble quieted down. "At least it'll keep me behind the stick," Kip had said when Edwards came calling again. The military, anyway, was thriving. Kip started pulling five, six high-altitude test runs a week, burning out the frustration on the very edge of space, refueling himself on pure ozone. The grin, the famous grin, had gotten tighter, but it had never faded. Or sold itself cheap.

She was showing the Uzbek minister how to trap M&M's inside a bubble of vodka when the buzzer sounded, the hatch opened, and Kumar came sliding in. The mood in observation suddenly brightened, the Luminaries all turning to one another giddily. Cady met Kumar's gaze, and for an instant he looked straight at her, frank and pleading: *Save me from these people.* Then the shine came back into his eyes, and he stretched a gala smile across his face. "Mr. Kumar, Mr. Kumar"—Benjamin practically fired himself across the cabin—"so thrilled you could join us. No shame in taking a moment to recuperate, no shame at all."

Finally, after ten minutes in which Cady could barely pay attention to anything the minister was saying, Kumar made it to her end of the cabin. The minister gave Kumar a slap on the back that sent him spinning like a top. "How you can be so graceful in space, Mr. Kumar?"

"I must say, Minister, you're right at home in microgravity yourself."

"No, oxen like me?" The minister thumped his own chest affectionately.

"When did we last see each other? Bukhara?" They chatted about various charity benefits. About Kumar's father and his notorious business acumen. "Oh, yes," Kumar said, "every nook and cranny for dear old Arnav." He couldn't have sounded wearier.

Across the cabin, the two tech billionaires were running diagnostics on one of their instrument arrays. The Chinese babe was throwing up again, this time, thank god, into a sealable bag. Cady gave her an *oh, honey* look, but couldn't tear herself away from Kumar.

"Well, shoot!" she said, breaking in on the minister. "How could I forget? Time to check Mr. Kumar's vitals. If you'll excuse us . . ."

They drifted to portside. "Thank you for that, truly." For a moment, Kumar seemed to lose himself in the spangled tableau out of the window. "How many trips is this for you?"

"Done all six," Cady said. "Plus forty in the module."

"You must be very good."

"Practically murdered myself." She gestured around the room. "But here we are."

Kip had never even given new-space a thought. Fantasy camp, he'd called it. After the accident, she'd tried to be stubborn too, had planned on staying with the Agency, even thought up about signing up for the Mars research, walling herself up in that mock capsule for the months on months of psych testing. Maybe they'd even have let her, poster child that she was. But when Nu-Luna's CEO called—*Cady, please, come see my Celestuary, give me notes*—she'd just folded. The whole time she wasn't sure if the dude wanted to hire her, fuck her, or put her in his museum. He'd shown off his collection of "government-era" memorabilia, claimed to know the history of the Agency backward and forward. Christ, he hadn't even heard Kip's name before.

"There was a storm over London as we were leaving orbit," Kumar said. "Really quite beautiful. To think it looks so grim down there." He grasped her arm, and she couldn't help shivering. "What was it like, your first time on the surface?"

How could she explain? She could tell him how moon dust shifted like snow under your boots, how with every step you were learning to walk again, that when you saw Earth hanging above the horizon you could hardly breathe, hardly form a thought, and that God—or the infinite, the faint echoes of the Big Bang, the dark flashes that seemed to lurk just behind all the visible universe, whatever—felt both impossibly distant and right up close. On the rock, she hadn't betrayed everything Kip stood for. Up there, she sensed him looming near.

"Honestly, it's . . ." She faltered, fell back on the company line. "There is no greater high. 'Awe-inspiring'? 'Once in a lifetime'? Don't do it justice. Not even your dreams can prepare you."

Kumar let go of her arm. Confusion passed over his face, and he suddenly seemed very young to her. "I can't wait. Really." He floated there, gazing desperately out into space. "Please, I may have a favor to ask of you."

"Always here to help. But what do you—"

The buzzer sounded. McPhee glided in, blinking and running a hand through his silvery hair. "Mr. Kumar! Heard you weren't feeling so hot. Launch bucks like a rodeo bull, don't it?"

McPhee went on, rattling off technical details, thrust ratios, burn rates, as if he and Kumar were two old space jocks. The crew was supposed to make the Luminaries feel "integral to the mission," but McPhee was laying it on. He had about as much subtlety as a vacuum toilet.

"Cady, what do ya say about that fudge swirl?" McPhee gave her a back-to-work twinkle of the eye, blinked several times, and turned again to Kumar. "Six days roundtrip, can't tell the tuna from the toothpaste. Fudge swirl's my one and only."

A boulder the size of a bank loomed before her. Fifteen feet up, she saw an outcropping, and before she knew what she was doing, she was rising toward it. It had been ten months since she'd last walked, and her panic was indistinguishable from her exhilaration. It was like hiking across a beach ball, the whole goddamn rock spinning underneath you, lofting you up. "I've, ah, lost visual on you." She tuned up a casual, unhurried drawl, knowing they were listening on Big Ambition, hoping she could buy some time. "Go ahead and report." Silence. Only the faintest static. "Okay, roger that, reading you now."

Against the powder gray terrain, she caught a quick glimpse of color, faded green and yellow and then a swath of red: the Brazilian and Chinese flags, hanging stiffly in the windless air. And then, dwarfing them both, Nu-Luna's purple banner—*The Next Giant Leap*—bright and bold with preformed ripples, to keep it from looking unnatural.

At twenty-eight hundred on the mission clock, it was all hands on lower deck. McPhee led the proceedings—more pep talk than final training session. Next to him, Cady stood in her EVA, waggling an arm or a leg as McPhee refreshed the Luminaries on the suit's corresponding systems. They looked on, wide-eyed. Compared to living quarters, lower deck was intimidating, cramped, bare-metal, warnings plastered on every bulkhead and hatch. You wanted to scare them a little. Otherwise, it didn't feel like the full ride. Around them, the other bulky white suits hung empty, chins on chests like melting snowmen.

"At the end of the day," McPhee was saying, "you got nothing to worry about. Ms. Cady'll keep you on the path, right beside you, every big, bouncing step of the way. And if you've been reading up on her, you know she's one of the last great public-sector cowgirls."

Cady silently groaned. She practically had McPhee's speeches—grand swathes of postnational, future-of-humanity stuff—memorized by now and tuned out for the rest, tried to think about her own prep for tomorrow's walk. But she couldn't help being distracted. Kumar was looking at her like a kid pressed against a toy store window.

For the rest of the day, everyone was nervy and restless. The two tech billionaires were driving everyone nuts handing out surveys with questions like, *On a lunar colony, would you expect (a) more laws, (b) fewer laws, or (c) everything will be judged strictly on a case-by-case basis, without reference to existing legal or moral codes, as in ancient Sumeria?* and laying out their instrument arrays like model train sets in every access point.

Finally, in the crew cabin, she tethered her sleeping bag to her bunk rail, zipped herself inside, drifted up near the ceiling—never could sleep strapped down. She closed her eyes, tried to get in a rest period. Six, seven minutes went by before she saw the first one: a quick zag of light like a scratch on a frame of film. Then, a few minutes later, several ghostly, asterisk-size explosions. Cosmic rays. Down on Earth, the atmosphere absorbed them. Up here, they were constantly slipping through your body. When they hit your retina, they made your rods and cones fire, made you see things that truly were not there. Another went off, tearing an orange streak across her lower vision. She squeezed her eyes tighter shut, but there was no stopping it. Finally, she wriggled out of her bag and slipped out into the gangway.

Big-A's humming and clicking seemed subdued, like it was lost in its own purple-hued dream. She felt heavy, tired, the dense, chill air parting around her like Jell-O. She tapped on the hatch to Kumar's cabin. No answer. She slowly turned the lock, sounding the buzzer.

His pillow floated like an errant thought above his bunk. She hesitated, took a quick sniff, then Velcroed the pillow to the wall. His sheets were damp and wrinkled; no one slept right up here. She watched the top sheet gently undulate.

Down on the lower deck, she found him inspecting the suits. "Hey," she called out softly. He flinched and spun around, a wild look on his face. But then the voice came forth, glossy and unperturbed: "Ah, you've caught me having a little preview." Still, he looked terrified.

She swallowed hard, not knowing what to say. She took up the empty sleeve of the suit. "You've seen the old brochures, the original designs? The company wanted glitz, but the first Luminaries hated it. They kept asking for the big old things from the Apollo days."

"You must think us horribly self-indulgent. Space tourists. Not up here for cause or country. Just to get our, I don't know, esoteric kicks."

"Well, you're doing this for your charity, right? To raise awareness about the orphans, their telecommunications needs."

"Oh, bullshit."

She smiled. He smiled back, a thin, fleeting thing like an apology.

"Traveling around like you do," she offered, "I bet you see a lot of need, a lot to fix."

"It's hard to believe, with no atmosphere, that these can protect you." Kumar gingerly felt the outside of the suit. "What if there was a leak? Or a puncture?"

"That won't happen."

"But if it did?"

"Here, let's give you more than a preview." She took him by the arm, propelled them both over to the ready area. "Slip out of those goddamn shiny pajamas."

He stripped down to his underwear, a pair of red and white briefs. She took in his taut, chiseled body. Plenty of time on his hands for exercise, it appeared.

"Okay, first things first. You remember this, don't you, big boy?" She handed him a purple adult diaper. "Some tech you just can't improve on." She helped him Velcro it on. He hung on to a rail, bobbing up and down, the lumpy, double-thick diaper an odd contrast to his smooth, dark skin. "Long undies next."

Watching him dress, her thoughts started spinning, pulsar-like, around a center. She and Kip had fantasized about it often enough: sex in zero Gs. Hell, late nights at the Outpost, it was all any AsCan could talk about. You joked, but, if you got up there, of course you'd try it. *I know what it'll be like*, Kip used to whisper in her ear. *It won't be friction, grinding together. It'll be like the tide coming in, waves lapping up the shore, closer, closer . . .*

"Now we get real fancy," she said, unfolding the undersuit from the locker, the feel of the soft, slick fabric making her shiver again. "A woven tricot Nylon layer, laced with cooling tubes"—she floated down and helped Kumar step into it, then came up the length of his body, cinching it tight—"designed to dissipate any . . . excess heat."

He swiveled his hips, testing the flex, ran his fingers over the webbed ridges of tubing. The look on his face—he was enthralled. *Or it'll be like falling up*, Kip would say. *Skipping right out of orbit, laughing, fighting for breath, spinning off into the infinite.*

She fit the communication cap over Kumar's head, handed him the cotton undergloves. She maneuvered the two of them over to where her own suit was fixed to the wall. "Get yourself into that lower assembly. Just shimmy right in there. That's it, get low." She pushed him down to his haunches, his lips just inches from her. "Now, come up through it."

Slipping her hands in between the two halves of the suit, she buttoned them up from the inside, feeling the muscle of his abdomen.

And when we come, Kip whispered, and they both broke into giggles, *the earth will move. But, you and me, we'll be way, way too high to feel it.*

"Cady," Kumar said, "is everything all right?"

"Sorry, it's . . . congestion." She swallowed hard again, sniffled. "All your fluids rise up here. Your head just doesn't know where it is."

She thought of the house in Houston, the empty bay in the garage, the two extra bedrooms now stacked with boxes, three if you counted the room that was going to be the nursery. *The next generation of AsCans.*

"So, tell me"—she put her hostess voice back on—"best vacation ever?"

Kumar looked away, flexing the gloves. "When I was eleven," he said, "my family went on holiday in Antigua. Or maybe it was Bali. I think I'd seen five continents by then. My mother was attending some embassy party. Diplomats, she loved diplomats. My father had to fly back to Delhi to settle another deal. And I was locked in our suite with a room service menu. I went out the window, managed to climb up onto the roof. And then I just sat there, staring at it. A gibbous, waxing, a time of good luck in India. Just massive. I was absolutely wild, couldn't contain myself. And then I jumped. In hospital, Mother had them dope me up, so I wouldn't cry. Three weeks in intensive care, I don't think I saw either of them more than a half-dozen times. But I dreamt about that moon constantly."

He flexed his fingers again, then reached out, played with the end of her ponytail, the individual strands waving with the currents of air, the calm breath of the ship.

"What's that favor you wanted to ask?" she said.

"Later." His face looked as hollow as a skull. "I wouldn't want to burden you."

"Here," she said, "one last thing, the helmet."

She slipped it off its hitch and brought it down over his head, swiveling it till it locked. Behind the visor, she could see his lips moving but only heard a muffled echo. She pointed to the knob on the right side of the helmet, the gold filter. He reached up and twisted it. His face disappeared, and she floated there, held by her own reflection in the dark curve of gold foil, her body stretching crazily out around him.

She took the rear, auxiliary hatch to the upper deck, up along the utilities array and past the steady whir of the carbon-dioxide scrubber. As she swung herself into the gangway, she heard someone digging around in the galley. She made to propel herself off the bulkhead, slip past unnoticed. Then she felt a tug at her foot: the billionaires' alkaloid meter, now tangled up in the Velcro of her right shoe. McPhee looked up from the stash he was raiding, a thin coating of freeze-dried ice cream on his lips. He drifted over, helped her extricate herself, blinking and rubbing at his eyes as he focused on the meter.

"Thought you were on rest period," he said.

"Just doing a few systems checks."

"That's an Agency jock for you. Always on the job."

He fired up some small talk about her old mentor at Johnson, acting like he knew the man when they'd only done a press conference together, back when Nu-Luna was splashing out on the Agency's pantheon, "special consultants," and scooping up the Dodos for monkey's pay. Finally, McPhee got her free of the billionaires' toy. She couldn't help scowling at the thing.

"Ms. Cady, we're a customer-forward team. Luminaries first, no matter what's happening with us on a personal level."

"Let them get their nap in, they'll be chipper by pre-walk brunch."

"Cady, look me in the eye."

"I think we're out of the Kobe sliders, but Benjamin will figure something out."

McPhee bulged his eyes. They were red and watery. "Tell me, what do you see?"

"What, the air a little dry? I'll adjust the humidity."

"Oh, fuck it, they're driving me crazy." McPhee touched his finger to his left eye, pulled it back. On the end of it sat a lens. "I've had a little deal going with the company doc. He's been writing me up 20/20, but now I need—" Pilot that he was, he couldn't bring himself to say *contacts*. "Point is, they'll be looking for someone."

"Well, shoot. Good luck, Jimson. No more safety checks for you."

McPhee made a sour face. "Jimson would not be my first recommendation."

It was as if she was suddenly breathing pure oxygen.

"I put you up for it," McPhee said, "they'll all be watching. CEO liked you from the get, but from now on everyone but everyone'll be dogging you. There's a board to answer to, shareholders. And you'll have to kiss some serious Luminary ass."

She could hardly follow McPhee. She was thinking instead of Kip, suited up for another flight at Edwards—routine, except nothing Kip did was routine. The Air Force footage played behind her eyes: Kip striding out to the runway, helmet under his arm, turning to the command tower, giving a thumbs-up as he climbed into the cockpit. His X-jet arrowing straight up, a whoop over the radio. God, he loved to redline that missile of a plane, bragged about it on their visits back to the Outpost, forlorn as they were, about blacking out, coming back around to alarms, warning lights, letting out another whoop on the radio. He'd always had something to give the Dodos a thrill.

"You've got a story of adversity," McPhee was saying. "Play it up. Nu-Luna could use a little press bump. And don't forget to mention your old captain now and then."

She just had the presence of mind to answer: "Guided me every step of the way, sir."

McPhee straightened up as if offended. "Kept you from flaming out more like."

"Practically a father figure to me."

"You know," McPhee said, pondering his contact, "it won't be the same up there—four, five years. That W they're building . . . hotel, spa, swimming pool, everything." He sighed. "To think, swimming in the Sea of Tranquility . . ."

The Agency had sent her to a therapist, who kept telling her to forgive Kip. Forgive him for what? This, right now, the chance to fly, wasn't this what they'd both always wanted?

"Goes without saying, this new development, just between you and me. Copy?"

"Sir, copy that." She'd only watched the Air Force footage once; it was seared into memory. Kip's black blur—an orange blur. In an instant. They never found out what went wrong. Could've been a hundred things. Ninety thousand feet up you didn't tailspin or disc or end over end. One bad twitch, you were particulate. Dust on the heavens. "Just you and me."

"Fine," McPhee concluded. "No need to salute or anything. Just get up to observation, help Benjamin clean up."

He went back to his ice cream, savoring his last taste.

In observation, Benjamin was yawning. The Luminaries were all sleeping or passed out. A spent pouch of Bud Light Altitude drifted across the cabin. "Well, look at you," Ben said.

She had no idea what her face was doing. She didn't know whether to laugh or cut loose with her own wild whoop or let hot tears dot the cabin. "Just can't wait to get out on the rock again."

"And where is Mr. Kumar?" Benjamin gave her a mock-scandalized look. "Because I know he isn't in his bunk."

"We were down below, giving him a sneak peek of tomorrow."

"Oh, lord," Benjamin said, "I bet you were."

Jimson's voice broke into her helmet. "Cady, you're way off leash."

"Just taking a stroll."

"Mr. Kumar isn't responding."

"He's a quiet guy. Didn't you notice?"

"Cady, this isn't procedure. You . . . protocol . . ." What sounded like a burst of static broke up the transmission. "Not something to be fucked—" Another burst, a loud crunch, then what sounded like a sharp in-suck of breath.

A piece of rock crumbled under her boot as she took the next leap, her stomach plunging with it. She barely made the rim of the crater. For a moment, she thought her suit must be malfunctioning, her visor must have swung down. Then she understood what she saw before her: an ocean, a continent, a hemisphere of shadow.

They went into orbit in the middle of McPhee's last big speech. The moon was exerting its first tug, anything unsecured now drifting to the floor. McPhee was listing names—Armstrong, Aldrin, Shepard, Conrad, Young, Perry—expounding on the proud tradition of those who'd walked before them and mentioning the heroes—the Chinese babe blushed—among them today. Kumar just stood there, wearing his bulletproof smile. "Before I quit blabbing here," McPhee was saying, "let me turn it over for a few words from the lovely Ms. Cady."

She looked at him, stunned. McPhee never passed up an opportunity to rhapsodize. With a courtly gesture, he directed her to the center of observation. She hardly knew what to say, just rambled for a couple of minutes, trying to remember the banter she'd worked on at Johnson. (Somehow Napoleon came back up.) She tried not to look at Kumar but couldn't resist. Maybe there was a way. She could climb back into her life. Kip would forgive her.

"The universe exploded out of a tiny little nothing. Reckon you can still hear it echoing. Can't even begin to tell you." She met Kumar's shining eyes. "Everything's new down there. Everything just starts right back at the beginning."

When Little Ambition touched down, it kicked up a mushroom of dust, and they had to wait for it to settle. She could see the Luminaries getting jumpy. The first two out were supposed to be Kumar and the

Chinese babe, but just as they were suiting up, the woman fainted. When she came around, she immediately broke out sobbing.

"It's common," Benjamin said. "Happens to the best of us. Take your time. Absolutely zero rush." He turned to the Interior minister. "Cady will take you out first. Okay? Everyone okay?" The minister nodded gravely, his mustache finally having settled into its official droop.

Cady helped Kumar into his suit, playing at the awkwardness of it but letting her hands linger. "It's everything you hope it is," she whispered to him. "Really, it is."

She slipped nimbly into her own EVA and sealed the helmet. "Fudge swirl"—her voice boomed back at her over the radio—"caramel pecan, Snickers crunch."

"Check," Benjamin said on Little Ambition.

"Check," Jimson said on Big Ambition.

"That's a check. Let's take a little stroll." She turned to Kumar, touched her helmet to his, the little ritual she and Kip used to do at Johnson. "Ready?"

Kumar's eyes shone. "I don't know how to thank you."

"Go ahead," she said. "No need to wait. It's time." As the outer hatch opened, she let him take the first step out onto the crater floor.

"Oh, my," he said. "At last."

She looked for the telltale columns of dust but could see nothing, only black plateau against black sky. She had the sudden, nauseating feeling of traveling at incredible speed. She turned on her shoulder lamp, opening a narrow alley of pocked and battered terrain, a sliver out of the darkness that spread all around her.

She closed her eyes, saw the footage, black blur, orange blur, dust on the heavens. Kip climbing into the cockpit, turning to command, giving the thumbs-up, his grin, his famous grin. He never would've stopped chasing it. Desk jobs, the nursery, the next generation of AsCans, *that* was the goddamn fantasy. Never would've been enough. Once you went up, down there just felt so leaden. The grin had never been for her. The drawl wasn't for him.

"Cady, come in!" Now McPhee was in her ear. "The hell's going on? Jesus, she's way off the goddamn path. Benjamin, get out there, bring in the minister!"

Her lamplight reflected off a thin cloud of settling dust. She set off toward it, gulping oxygen. Before her, what looked like arrowheads glinted obsidian and gold across a jutting rock. It took her a moment to understand what they were—shards of Kumar's visor.

"Roger that? Cady?!" McPhee was yelling. "There'd better be a damn good—"

She took a deep breath, drew in the smell of ozone. He was close. Up here, it was all so close. She reached for her control box, turned off her radio and lamp, and took another leap.

BLACK CAR

The snow had started early that morning, and the wind was bad and so was the cold. Still, he'd been waiting on the radio all day. "You sure?" dispatch said when he responded. "They're talking shutdown on 65. Plus, she's at the dirty dog."

"Her card clear?"

"Yeah, I ran it."

The pickup was going north to Chicago, four hours straight up through the storm. But he needed the job. "We'll get there," he said.

He drove one of the service's smaller cars, a black Crown Vic. He got the engine running, scraped the windshield, settled into the leather seat that took his bulk with a creak and a soft release of air. Then he was out into the gray, swirling day, aiming for downtown Indy and the Greyhound station.

The pickup was a girl, seventeen, eighteen, dark hair in a tight ponytail, backpack slung over her shoulder. He got out, took the pack, nestled it in the popped trunk. "What you got there?" the girl asked, pointing to a gleam of polished wood peeking out from the folds of an old quilt. Earlier, he'd wrapped up the clock, tucked it between the spare and the wheel well, so he could deliver it that night. "Cleaning house," he murmured. "Out with the old."

She went around to the front passenger side.

"You'd be more comfortable in back?"

"I'll watch the snow," she said. "At least it's pretty."

He got on the highway. The girl talked about how boring the bus up from Tallahassee had been. She should've taken a pill, conked right out. But then she'd probably be snoring in that station, waiting out the storm like everyone else. More than an hour she'd tried to get a car on her phone.

"The amateurs aren't out today," he said.

In less than a year, business had dropped by half. He'd looked at getting on the app. But they were screening harder now. He was lucky the service even kept him on.

Five miles up 65, they hit traffic barrels and a state trooper waving everyone off to the exit. They got on the county road, passed a semi jackknifed in the ditch.

"Uh oh," she said.

"Some of these truckers, rate they hire them, it's bumper cars out here."

She let out an abrupt, high-pitched laugh. It startled him, and the road briefly shuddered under his hand. But she only yawned and leaned against the window. He thought of his daughter. Same age almost. The girl was carefully made up. But her hair was greasy, cheeks hollow. She'd been on the road more than Tallahassee.

"I was down Florida way once. Neptune Beach. Honeymoon," he added, surprising himself by volunteering this. "You get your time in the sun?"

She smiled at him, tight and quick. "Hey, sorry if I . . . Maybe some music?" Before he could, she reached over, turned on the radio.

An AM station came on. "You have wallowed, you have bathed yourself in sin and—" He jabbed at the button. Top 40 roared on.

The girl seemed satisfied, hummed along. He focused again: the centerline disappearing, reappearing under the snow snaking across the road, the drifts piling against the slat roadside fences, miles of stubbled corn, Hackelman, Gas City, Banquo. The heat slowly drained out of his cheeks. Getting caught on that preacher station. But he liked their admonishments, the way they accused you, beat you up some before they told you to come back in.

He'd last spoken to his wife seven months ago. Three weeks before that, he'd moved out in a rush, just stuffed anything into the trunk of the Crown Vic. She'd come to his by-the-week apartment for the clock, a mantelpiece, real walnut, given to her by her dad, an heirloom meant to pass down. He'd said he didn't have it. They'd screamed at each other. Now he was bringing it back to her. He could still come back in.

Next to him, he heard the girl softly snore. She'd slipped out of her coat, had it pillowed against the window. He remembered the night of his daughter's seventh grade dance. Back then, he'd driven a stretch. He'd put on his uniform, cap and everything. Listening to his daughter and her friends laugh and gossip over the Cokes he'd stocked in the little fridge, he never knew he could be so happy. Underneath her white T-shirt, one of the girl's nipples was showing. He reached to nudge up the heater. She let out another snore, stirred half-awake. He blinked, looked back at the road.

A pickup coming around the bend ahead blasted its horn. Its back end fishtailed. The truck began to spin. Jack stepped on the gas, yanked the wheel to the right. The truck slid by them, went off the road, and thumped into a snow drift. The Crown Vic hit the shoulder. He gripped the wheel hard, didn't brake. The car jerked back onto the road. He eased them to a stop. The radio played distantly. He felt his heartbeat in his fingertips.

"Shit," she said, hyperventilating, "shit, shit, shit."

"You all right?"

"I'm, yeah, shit, I'm . . ."

He turned off the ignition, stepped out into the brittle cold. "Be right back."

A gaunt old guy in tan overalls was climbing down from the truck. Jack marched over to him, clutching his keys. The world began to lean sideways, that old, queasy feeling. He saw himself smashing his fist into the guy's wind-chapped cheek. He squeezed harder. The keys' teeth bit. Slowly, the world righted itself.

"Want a tow?" he rasped out. "I'll call it in. But they're probably working overtime." What he couldn't do was a report, another strike on his record. He'd maneuvered them all out of a wreck. He might have drifted over the line too.

The old guy glanced up and down the road. "Let's see I can't back it out first."

The girl was out of the car. She came up beside him, huffing breath into her hands as they watched the truck churn its tires in the drift. But the old guy got it out, climbed down again to inspect. Big, ugly dent in the front bumper. Shit, Jack thought. Next would be insurance. The road started to slide out from under him.

The old guy looked at him, frowned—and the girl stepped forward. "Day like this," she said, "you'd think we wouldn't be rushing. But I haven't seen my boys in, what, three weeks? I guess you take any dumb risk."

The guy tucked his hands up under his armpits, seemed to consider. Then he said, "I was out after hot cocoa for my Lucia. Certifiable. How old your boys?"

"Three, seven, little monsters." The girl smiled, somewhere between flirting and consoling. "Fetching hot cocoa in a whiteout, you must be in the first blush."

"Going on forty-one years," the old guy said.

"She don't even have to put you on the leash!"

"That's about it."

The girl laughed again, but this time beautiful, silvery, like wind in the branches of an iced-over tree.

Back on the road, he took it slow. The snow had turned fat and steady, splotching the few passing headlights orange. "Thanks for that," he said. "Back there."

"You steered us out of one bad development."

"I need to apologize. Customer safety is job one and—"

"Enough on that." She wrapped her arms around herself, shivered. "I can't listen to men play humble. You saved our butts."

He felt more words pressing out. "Three and seven, huh? What are their names?"

The girl—but he guessed now maybe she wasn't—hauled her coat back on. "Carter and Braydon. Monster one, monster two."

He laughed, but she just shivered again. They went on in silence. His thoughts jumped around, still scattered by the close scrape: His daughter, at seven, running around in a snowstorm, tongue poked out, giggling her head off. Neptune Beach, his wife's hands, cool lotion on his sunburned back, rolling around on that motel bed, not caring about the burn. The nights he'd slept in the back of the Crown Vic, his sweat getting into the seats. And that blinding bright day, downtown Indy, three years back, the idiot who'd broadsided him, totaled the Lincoln he'd once driven. Jack had shoved away the airbag, the mangled door, tumbled across the wildly tilting street. Then he was yanking the driver out of his car, hitting and hitting him, the other man's face turning something strange.

"Hey," the girl said, "you hungry?" She reached up, batted the little cardboard pine tree hung from the rearview. "Think that's a diner open back there. Shit, I haven't had a real bite since Florida. And we could use a break, right?"

They'd just passed through Morocco, making good time, maybe getting ahead of the storm. But, day like this—no, rushing didn't help. He turned around in a driveway leading to a tumbledown grain silo. "Sure," he said, "a little breather."

The diner was empty except for the waitress and the cook, who were both sitting at the counter watching some baseball movie. "Anywhere," the waitress said. He and the girl took a booth. She ordered a hot meatloaf sandwich, mashed potatoes, clam chowder, orange soda. He asked for coffee, a chef salad. "Cholesterol," he explained.

"I like a man eats a steak," the girl said.

"Yeah, screw it, steak and eggs," he said to the waitress. "Medium-rare, over-easy." He unclipped his tie, undid his top button. Some situation, eating with a client. He couldn't stop seeing her as a girl. "You put people at their ease," he said. "I can tell."

"That's nice," she said, smiling as she sucked on her orange soda. "Thank you."

"It's a good trait to have. One of the best."

Daughter, he wanted to say. My daughter. Instead, he waved at the TV. "My dad used to be an umpire. Minor leagues, all over the Midwest. Called a thousand games."

"Oh, yeah, was he fair?"

"Well, we liked him better when he was on the road."

"I wouldn't do it," she murmured. "All those folks screaming at you."

Yes. Exactly. All the idiots blasting their horns, playing with their phones, never looking, never even thinking where they were going. And they let these people keep on, deadly weapons between their hands. It got into you. How many scrapes had he seen? How many wrecks? Had to get it out somehow. She'd listen. The warmth of the words gathering—he must have been blushing again. He'd just start telling her.

Outside, the snow was falling only faintly now. They watched it.

"Maybe I should've rode it out down in that crappy bus station," she said.

"This holds up," he mumbled, "we're maybe an hour out."

"Man, best thing I've heard all day."

The waitress took away their plates. He insisted on paying. "To make up for that close scrape," he said. She thanked him, said she had to step out, make a call. She wanted to check in with her sister, her boys, tell them she was almost home.

After Gary, the roads were cleared and salted. The Skyway was open, and they had it to themselves, the whole stretch arcing way above the grimy plants and slumped bungalows. A buoyant feeling came upon him. He was excited for her and her family, that moment she came through the door. He'd linger a minute, just to see that. With I-65 plowed, he'd be back in Indy in time to catch his wife after dinner. He could find the road back.

They came off the Skyway, down to the city proper. He glanced over at her. She blinked several times, as if seeing him for the first time. He thought again of his daughter, just about to go to nursing school, studying to take care of people. When he was younger, he'd wanted to be a firefighter, even took the course, worked volunteer for a year. But the driving—you were always sitting, getting too fat and slow to go up a ladder, still getting home exhausted, all that rage stalled out, stifled, always delivering other people, never arriving yourself. Everyone who got injured, got maimed out here—maybe his daughter would one day take good care of them.

"Excuse me," the girl said, "could we pull off here?"

"Sure. Gas station? Need the bathroom?"

"Maybe just take this exit."

He turned off the highway and on to a frontage road with a car wash, a big hardware store, a Chinese buffet. "Turn in here," she said. The parking lot of a closed down bank, its windows all papered over, scaffolding around all four sides. But the sign for the bank was still lit up, bright blue and green. He stopped in the middle of the lot.

"You don't want to be dropped here, do you?"

She shook her head, kneaded her hands in her lap. "Listen," she began, "I'm just trying to get home to my kids."

The heat came back into his cheeks.

"I've only got thirty bucks on me. And this ride is, what, three hundred?"

"But your card cleared," he said in a strangled voice.

"I called and cancelled it back at that diner. Everything else is maxed out." She laughed. The silver was gone. "I was hoping we could work something out."

He looked in the rearview, saw his tire tracks in the fresh snow. On the frontage road, a wine-red Chrysler with rusted fenders moved silently, gray exhaust following. She touched his leg and held her hand there.

"They're far away," she said. "They don't see. No one sees driving by."

He put his own hand lightly on top of hers. He followed the progress of the Chrysler. Finally, it disappeared. He looked down, his hand on top of hers, nearly twice the size, her dry, chapped knuckles against his sweating palm.

"What do you like?" she said. "Just tell me."

"No, I—"

He wanted to say something, to reassure her, a girl, a young parent. But he couldn't even look her in the eyes. He picked up her hand, gave it back to her, took his own away. He reached up and put the car into gear.

"You don't have to pay." The words came out hoarse, ragged. "I'll tell dispatch it was because of that close scrape. Customer accommodation."

He'd have to fill out an incident report. It'd been his call to drive today, and now he'd have to tell dispatch he'd nearly wrecked. After that, he didn't know what.

"I can't tell you what it means," the girl said. "I've been traveling so long."

"I'll take you home," he said.

He merged back onto the highway. After a few miles, she told him to exit into a neighborhood of vinyl-sided bungalows, told him which turns to make. He still wanted to tell her something good. But the memory that rose up: the night he'd come home from driving, wrists, back, head aching, found his daughter emptying a bottle of ketchup all over the new carpet, his wife on the phone in the other room the whole time. What happened next—how could he explain to her? The world had taken a very long time to right itself.

"I drove a guy home from the hospital once," he began. "Him and his girlfriend. He'd been in a coma for three weeks, motorcycle crash. I guess he wanted to go home in style. I told them, 'Don't worry about the tip.'"

No, no—not that. Why that?

"Bet they appreciated it," she murmured and told him to pull up to a bungalow with two separate driveways, two front doors. The left half was dark. The right had a light on. He put the Crown Vic in park. Out of the car, it was face-hurt cold but pristine, the kind of clean feeling you got after big snow. He took her backpack from the trunk.

"Thanks again for lunch." She cradled the backpack. "You didn't have to."

"For that close scrape," he said again. Some reassurance—he could at least give her that, tell her there was always a road back. They stood in the cold another moment.

"Drive safe," she said, walked to the front door, and went inside.

He paced the length of the car, snow squeaking under his shoes. He listened for voices, someone running up to greet her. Instead, there came a dull thunk—something falling, being dropped. Immediately, he stepped toward the door, keys in his fist. But then he stood frozen, rage beating uselessly through him.

He stood in the cold until it was a dull, distant thrum. Then he popped the trunk again, took out the clock, set it on the front step of the bungalow. He got back into the Crown Vic, slumped in the seat, leather creaking under him, engine idling through his bones. He dropped the car into reverse. Then he just sat with his foot on the brake. Minutes went by. He just sat there, holding tight to the wheel.

DECOYS

It was my first summer at the Lighthouse. Working the night shift was a local dirtbag rite of passage. Long, dry-eyed, dusty hours, the numb repetition of breaking down loads off the trucks, stacking and facing shelves, can after can, box after box, bottle after bottle, all for bare minimum wage and the rare, stingy, nothing customer tip. Yeah, of course we ran wild.

After close, when the cashiers had counted out and punched out, we grabbed armfuls of Pillsbury biscuit dough, the tall cans that *pop* when you twist, set them up ten in a triangle, and hauled Butterballs over from frozen. Gruetz and Stauffacher, who'd both flunked off varsity hockey, could one-arm those mothers. The rest of the night crew—floor guy, Divorced Dave, Ramirez Uno, Ramirez Dos—bowled granny style. Buffed tile + melting poultry + regelation right at the phase boundary = goddamn velocity. But forget getting a strike, we were all just waiting to see what Mays would do.

He clutched the plastic-wrapped turkey to his uniform polo, right over the Lighthouse Food Wine Liquor logo, and squinted down the aisle, rocking side to side.

"What, you gonna rail it or something?!" Gruetz mimed something depraved, sniffed his finger, pinched his nose, and crowed, "Minky stinky! Minky stinky!"

Mays blinked and trembled. His folks used to run a mink barn down by the county line. Back in middle school, I'd see Mays driving around with his dad, rounding up carcasses from the dairies, piling up the truck bed to feed those tiny-teeth minks. There was good money in pelts, low costs, but the smell was piss city. Kids would hold their noses when Mays passed by in the hall in his camo hoodie. When Gruetz and Stauffacher did it now, it still chirped him right up.

"Don't," Mays muttered. "Don't even—"

"Minky fucking stinky!"

Mays stopped trembling, went rage red. He hinged over, swung the turkey once, twice, and—hurled it into the baby food shelves. Mini jars of pureed yams and creamed beef came raining down. We busted right up. "Mays, man! Absolute goon!"

Ocampo, the night manager, all goatee and acne pits, just barked a laugh. Corporate was too tight to pay for CCTV or do a real inventory, so he didn't sweat a little slippage. "All right, clean it up." He flicked a finger at Mays and then, shit, me.

"Yeah, thanks, Ocampo," Mays said as we contemplated the glass-studded goop. Like he himself hadn't just caused the mess.

"Toss these?" I held up a couple of jars that only had dented lids. "Mark them damaged?"

"Jesus, Hart," Mays said between gritted teeth, "what you asking me for?"

At the end of the aisle, Gruetz and Stauffacher were snickering like lawn sprinklers. I was the fucking new guy, a year past graduation, still saving for tech school, the few pals I'd had gone off to UW–Platteville and Superior, and now Ocampo had paired me with the psycho. Mays had called me Hart, not Shart like everyone else did, but I couldn't help myself.

"Hey, man," I said, hard enough to travel, "at least I showered today."

Big laugh from the end of the aisle. Mays just winced, murmured, "Toss 'em." In the overhead fluorescent glare, I saw he was wearing . . . makeup around his eye. He caught me staring, turned away. "And get a mop already."

The cherry blossoms, the dunes, the lighthouses, the view from the bluffs as Lake Michigan sprawls out endlessly, placid and steely clear and haunted by shipwrecks bleached birch gray—they say Door County is the prettiest place within a five-hour drive of Chicago.

That summer, I barely saw it. Working nights, I'd wake up four, five in the afternoon, dazed, dislocated. Distantly, I'd hear my pop down in the basement, the soft *chunk* of his chisel biting into white cedar as he carved yet another decoy. It was practically his sole pursuit since he'd gone on workman's comp, his right eye milky blind from a splinter flung off the lathe.

I'd pull on my Lighthouse shirt, wolf whatever leftovers Mom had foil-wrapped, blink out the sleep over one of my fat pop-physics paperbacks. Our house was the only one on the road occupied through the week and the winter. Mom was always off mowing the flatlanders' grass, watering their gardens, picking up after their parties. I'd spend an hour reading Hawking or Penrose or Feynman, then call down to my dad, "Heading out!"

"Ride safe," he'd call softly back. And then I'd get on my Huffy and skirt along Baileys Harbor, staring off at the old lighthouse on Cana Island still beaming out across the lake as I winged past the mansions and the speedboats chopping the waves, my head off working the principle of least action and infinite series equations. And then I'd go through the sliding doors and into the polar embrace of the store AC and try to forget it all for the space of a shift.

One night, we were playing backroom ball, doing sky hooks and dunks with a ball of pallet wrap and a hoop made of baling wire. Mays banged through the door flaps, humping flats of Robin Hood flour. "The hell back to work," he muttered. "Be here till dawn." Despite everything, Mays worked like a demon. We'd been in the same class, though Mays had dropped out senior year to go full-time. He was set on making assistant manager.

"Got a date?" Gruetz hollered at him. "Christina finally give in?!" Christina was one of the cashiers. Thirty-one, and her mom still dropped her off. Back then, we'd have called her slow. Well, we said worse than that. "Oh, oh, Christina! Suck my minky pinky . . ."

On cue, Mays went into his quivering rage, only he seemed frozen in it. Stauffacher bounced the pallet-wrap ball off his head. He didn't even flinch. Then suddenly he screamed, a wordless guttural thing, and dropped the stack of flour. The yellow sacks busted open. Fine white powder puffed up. Mays stood blinking inside it while we all cracked up.

He picked up an unbroken sack, slit it open with his cutter, and hurled it. It hit Gruetz square in the chest and exploded. Gruetz hunched into himself, like on the hockey ice before a brawl, an instant away from beating Mays's skinny little ass. We all hung on the edge of it, maybe longing for Mays to finally get pounded into goulash. And then I reached for the half-open sack and slung it up into the big ceiling fan, covering the whole room in white.

"Merry Christmas!" Gruetz cried, and we went into a frenzy, winging sacks of flour at one another, laughing, shouting, skating around on it. At one point, I glanced over at Mays. He gave me a quick nod, rubbed at his face, and I saw what I'd missed before, a bruise haloing his eye like the rot around the bite in an apple.

We'd all seen Mays's dad stumbling out of the Blue Ox in the middle of the afternoon. After Mays's mom left—went off with some Chicago Board of Trade guy who summered up here—his dad had poisoned the whole barn, tried to call it mink flu to get the insurance payout, and nearly landed himself in lockup. That was, what, two, three years ago? The old farmhouse by the county line had gone to hell. Mays was probably paying the mortgage, but it looked like his dad was whipping on him too.

Mays grabbed a broom. I snapped another handle into a wide, shaggy head, and we went around together, side by side, sweeping up the flour. "Hey," I said, "I'm real sorry."

"About what?"

"No, right, it's just . . . You shouldn't have to . . ." I gestured at his eye.

His lips parted, but he didn't answer. He just hunched his shoulders, focused on the broom head as we went around the warehouse, turning the floor from white back to gray.

In the run up to Memorial Day, we worked thirteen-hour shifts, straggled out when the day crew came in. They didn't know that we'd done half of it wearing Depends on our heads, that Stauffacher had been trying for weeks to fart over the PA, mixing himself a cocktail, "Door County Dynamite," of sauerkraut, clam, and pickled onion juice, creaking the gooseneck into position, letting a pause linger, then muttering, "Not again."

Day of the holiday, a half hour before close, Ocampo came on the intercom. *Spot check on milk. Immediate spot check, milk.* We knew what that meant: hot chick, dairy department. Gruetz, Stauffacher, Divorced Dave, and I ran over and peered around the dog food endcap. She was twenty-six, twenty-seven, hair a glossy waterfall down to the crack of her jean shorts, cowboy boots so new the leather creaked. (For some reason, Chicago people dressed all country up north.) She was talking on a chunky cell phone, the first I'd seen outside *L.A. Law*, and saying, "What? Kahlua? No, liquor's closed. I know, I know. They shut it early up here."

Ocampo was pretending to tidy a Crystal Pepsi display. He shook his head—always liquor with these people. Illinois sold late, Wisconsin was all Lutheran, and the country club jagoffs jawed us out when they couldn't get beer on a Saturday night. But the city girls—their offhand, obliterating beauty—were almost worse. They showed us just how backwoods we were. I felt Gruetz and Stauffacher already itching to get away. All we *could* do was look.

And then Mays came knocking through the swinging doors, whistling some ditty, and started filling the skim. He made like he'd just noticed her. "Help ya find anything?"

"I was looking for Kahlua? Liquor section's closed?"

"Oh, yeah, state ordinance. Serious pain in the keister."

"Any substitutes?"

Mays pondered, as if he'd ever drunk anything stronger than Old Mil or DC Dynamite. "Nah, can't beat Kahlua. Warms ya right up, don't it?"

The girl smiled at him curiously. "Sure."

"We'll get you straighten care of. Meet me round back."

The girl smiled again—annihilating—and whispered, "Got it."

The rest of us rushed to the loading dock. A BMW pulled down the alley. Mays opened the receiving door. The night was quiet, just her car idling expensively. She rolled down her window. Mays slipped her the bottle. "Wow," she said, "what do I owe you? Can I pay card?"

Mays waved it off. And then he risked it. "Where you hanging tonight?"

"Oh, I . . . just with some friends at the cabin."

"Baileys Harbor? Love it over there."

"Just a little getaway. Tiny thing."

Silence swirled in the air between them. "Need anything else"—Mays proffered a scrap of paper—"call here. Special delivery. Any time."

"Hey, thanks. Sorry—" She dug in her purse for a bill. "This is really all I have."

"Oh, no." It was enough to make Mays start rubbing at his eye. "Any time, any time."

She purred off into the night, and Mays came back into the stockroom, blinking against the buzzing lights. I thought to offer something—Check out the stones on Mays!—and kept expecting Gruetz or Stauffacher to jump in: Don't sweat it, Christina'll still blow you! But we all just stood there, Mays trembling slightly, lips pursed in an almost whistle.

"All right, dicksnaps," Ocampo finally said, "back to work."

I had the next day off, tried to catch up on sleep. All I could hear was the soft chunk, chunk, chunk of my pop in the basement. I went down softly, so as not to startle him, but he turned, looked me over with his milky eye, beckoned me to sit. I took a stool next to him, watched him shaping the mantle of a preening northern pintail, his good eye twitching with every blow of the chisel, the other unflinching. "Well," he finally said, "something's got up you."

I thought about telling him that two days ago I got called up to sack a late order. Four goddamn carts, about thirty little tubs of Häagen-Dazs in there, and this lady telling me, Don't crush the rolls, don't crush the rolls! Then she wants propane, then ice, and by the time we get out to her SUV the size of an Abrams tank, it's all melting, she's scowling, doing nothing to help, doesn't want to chip her nails, saying, You call this "full service"? Right ma'am, sorry, ma'am, fuck you, ma'am, and before I closed the trunk—she's already in the driver's seat, revving exhaust in my face—I reached in, tossed a couple of Häagen-Dazs under the tire well. Smell that in the morning, ma'am. God, I wanted to unload about it. But my mom's whole job was putting up with flatlanders. And something about that milky eye of his made it impossible for me to bitch around my pop.

"About halfway to what I need for Sturgeon Tech," I told him. "Or, I don't know, MATC? Platteville? Or I could get on at the tool and die, learn some CAD."

"Hmm," he said and nodded for me to reach him a rasp.

All around us, on shelves high and low, beady-eyed ducks stared out. He was supposed to sell them, less to hunters than summer people looking to decorate, but just kept piling them up instead. Who knew how long the workman's would last? And Mom couldn't mow lawns forever. I'd have to support them, and doing that from Door County felt like a life sentence. Hard to resent the man. He'd punched a clock before it'd punched him, but his lousy depth perception meant even his most beautiful decoys were misshapen. Still, that milky eye saw things.

"Know what they all get wrong?"

"What?" I was suddenly desperate for wisdom, encouragement, anything.

"They put out forty, fifty crappy plastic birds, think they'll pull down a whole flight."

"Oh," I said, "right."

"Or they go for the real thing"—he indicated his white cedar pintail—"but cheap out, like one is gonna do it. One duck on the water, what's that gonna do?"

"Yeah." I truly didn't know. "Dumbass flatlanders."

"One duck floating brings the foxes. Scares them all off."

"Got it." I heard, Don't go off on your own. Fly with the flock. "Hey, thanks, Pop."

His milky eye roved over me. Then he wrinkled his brow, replied with another "hmm," and went back to his northern pintail.

Mays was punching in, Lighthouse cap pulled down low over his eyes. "Yo, goon!" I winged a ball of pallet wrap at him. He batted it away, but it dislodged his cap, and I saw the welt on his forehead, ugly and plum-purple.

"Jesus," I said, "you okay?"

He just pushed past me, disappeared into the freezer. I thought he'd stay in there the whole shift, busting his knuckles on fish sticks and Klondike Bars. But on my fifteen, he came into the break room, sat heavily across from me. I was reading *Popular Science*. He had *Outdoor Wisconsin*, a camo-clad bow hunter at full draw on the cover. "Sweet," I said vaguely.

Mays reached for his wallet, slid an overexposed photo across the table: mom and dad posing in the pickup bed, holding up an eight-pointer by its antlers, sunset flaming behind the mink barns. And little Mays: feet dangling, grinning, twenty-gauge cracked over his knee. Even I knew it wasn't a trophy buck, but I said, weirdly downhome, "Who took *that* monster?"

"I winged him!" Mays all but yelped. "Mom took him. Right through both lungs."

I wanted to ask: When'd you see her last? Your dad ever going to let up on you? And why don't you just knock the old fuck out? Instead, I stayed quiet.

"Straight through," Mays went on. "She taught me, be patient. Deer hears as good as a dog. One snapped branch—gone! See?" He mimed raising a rifle, a millimeter at a time. "Real, real slow. Hunting ain't violence, it's patience. Damn. She was better than any of us."

"Matt," I said, using his first name. "Man, I'm sorry. I mean . . . it sucks. It all sucks."

He looked up, touched the welt, flinched. "It's just, down in Chicago, I went down there to see her. But she . . ." He started blinking furiously. "I'm not sure she even wanted to think about coming back up—"

Just then Stauffacher burst in and lunged for the PA mic. He crooked it, held it to his crack, strained purple in the face. Nothing. "Why?!" Stauffacher cried and stamped back out.

We ground through the Fourth, the pea-soup weeks that followed, the air thick with mosquitoes, with the stifled energy of an overripe summer. August was coming, and though I had enough for the first tuition payment, I still hadn't enrolled at Sturgeon Tech or even applied. I couldn't think about any of it. Gruetz discovered the keys to the florist's counter, and we used their birthday-balloon helium to squeak out our voices and send inflated condoms drifting around the store. Before close, we'd bring choice items up to check-out to gross out the cashiers: turkey baster, gerbil food, KY Jelly. End of shift, we'd hang around the parking lot while Ocampo did neutral drops in his Monte Carlo, his carburetor shredding the early morning silence before he fishtailed right into the adjacent cornfield. None of it made $5.35 an hour seem any higher.

Mays had started hanging back from all of it, angling for promotion, trying not to screw up. The guys just provoked him all the more. Gruetz propped an open gallon of milk on top of the swinging doors, called him back to the stockroom. Mays barreled right through, got himself soaked. Then Ocampo gave him a note to read over the intercom: *Mr. Keydick, please come to customer service. First name Don. Mr. Don Keydick, to customer service.* Mays read it twice, then broke off, and went and worked the freezers. One night, as he and I were stocking pickles, Stauffacher came cruising down the aisle on the power jack. He executed it perfectly, an upward bending, quizzical fart, right in Mays's face. I waited for it: Mays going truly apeshit. Stauffacher nearly fell off the jack laughing. I started to echo him, but then I thought about that lady—You call this "full service"?—about the day I'd dicked around in physics coming up with a TI-83 program to solve relative velocity problems. I'd shown Mrs. Stevens. Where'd you get that from? she'd said and wrote me up for cheating. I thought maybe she was right. They were all right about us.

Mays just closed his eyes, let out a breath, and went on shelving the Vlasic Kosher.

Three nights later, I was half home when my Huffy blew a tire. I started pushing in the two AM dark, mosquitos feeding all over me, too tired to even swat them away. I saw the old lighthouse off in the distance, its beam sweeping across the night. I knew why so many people drove up here to see it, why, obsolete, it never got torn down. It made you feel lonesome and lost, like a ship feeling its way across the endless inland ocean. From a nearby inlet, I heard ducks gabbling and, off in the cavern of my skull, felt my pop's chisel going chunk, chunk, chunk. I remembered Feynman writing, "The first principle is that you must not fool yourself," and pictured the curve of Lake Michigan like a parabola and me on an asymptote that would never ever converge. As I trudged along the shoulder, shins knocking my pedals, a vehicle rumbled up beside me and honked, and I braced myself to get hit with a beer can or something. But it slowed and pulled over—Mays's rusted-out pickup, the one he and his dad once piled up with carcasses. He cranked down the window, called out in a cracking voice, "Yo, Hart! Get in already."

I tossed my bike in the back, and we took off. After a few minutes, I saw that we weren't aimed toward town and my house, and I figured we were just cruising, like you did in Door County. I thought about telling Mays that Ocampo had taken me aside the other night, said, "Assistant job coming open. You interested?" But now was not the time. Maybe we were heading to Mays's place, the farmhouse. I thought I might just have to punch his dad out myself. Then Mays took the turn for Baileys Harbor, and I could only say, "Holy goddamn hell."

Mays's grin practically glowed in the dark. "Special dee-livery."

We churned down a gravel road. Out on the horizon, heat lightning was flashing, like some war being fought over the deep water. Every time we hit a bump, a flurry of rattling and clinking came from the trunk. Mays must have loaded up on the liquor. His ticket to Shangri-La, and he was letting me ride shottie. I felt his nerves giddying the air. Every couple of minutes, he reached for a small bottle of Binaca on the dash and spritzed his mouth menthol. "Angie," he said, and I guessed that was Kahlua's name, "is a total sweetheart, actually."

We chunked and rattled over another bump. Mays's truck scraped its exhaust, sounded like it'd shake itself to pieces; I already felt embarrassed to arrive like this. More lightning lit up the waves rolling into the harbor, the dunes and pines, bleached out even the old lighthouse's beam. At the end of the promontory sat a warmly lit cabin. There were nine, ten vehicles, BMWs, open-topped Jeeps. Mays's truck grumbled to a stop. He reached into the glove, sprayed his pits with Lynx, then unscrewed the lid of some beige cream and started daintily concealing the remnants of his shiner in the rearview. I watched him in silence, then started to climb out. He grabbed me by the sleeve of my polo.

"Jesus, Hart," Mays said, "lose the uniform."

Walking up to the cabin, we were both in white undershirts, black slacks, and black shoes, looking like Mormons or fugitives, humping enough liquor to make a priest nervous. Just as we came up on the porch, I caught a whiff of . . . dead perch washed up on shore? No, it was me. Earlier, at the store, we'd been fish jousting. You took a whole salmon or trout from seafood, wrapped and wrapped it in plastic, then slugged each other until it all just went to pieces. I reeked, wanted to hold my own nose. Mays freed a finger from around a box of Jack Daniels, rang the bell. The door swung open. A guy in cargo shorts squinted out. "Delivery's here!"

My blood churned. That's all we were: delivery boys. And then Kahlua blazed up to the door, flamed round by the light of the party. "Oh, wow, you came."

"Totally," Mays said. "What's up, Angie? Great to see you."

"Yeah! Likewise! Sorry, can't remember . . . Do you take card?"

Mays flushed red, then paled. "Oh, I didn't . . . You really don't have cash?"

Angie shrugged adorably, like she was forgiving *us*. "We took a collection, but . . . no one uses it in the city."

We were carting maybe three weeks' salary. That much liquor gone missing would get management shouting. Mays would have to pay it back, work it out with Ocampo so, best case, they didn't can his ass. I could see all of this flicker across his face. As casually as he could, he said, "On the house."

"I can get out more tomorrow."

"Totally on the house."

We stood on the threshold, the guy in cargo shorts eyeing us. Because she had to now, Angie invited us in. There were twenty, twenty-five guests, half in Ralph Lauren, half in country and western. Some were lounging on rattan sofas and armchairs, a bunch were gathered round a ping-pong table, playing beer pong. Mays and I deposited the liquor on the kitchen island, and the guys came over like moths to a zapper. Somewhere in there, Angie mixed us both drinks, and *we* said, "Thanks," and Mays started peppering her with questions. She said something about law school. Most of them were law students. They'd all met in Evanston. The cabin was her parents' place. Her mom had been born up here. One last blowout before the new quarter. I felt all elbows and salmon stink, sipped then gulped my Jack and Coke, and thought this cabin could be one my mom cleaned. Tomorrow morning, she'd be down on hands and knees scrubbing right where I stood.

I watched the beer pong, and slowly I realized that the guys, despite the sporty clothes, were reedy and pale. They were dorks. And the girls, even Angie, had a flyaway look, not enough time, not even enough money, yet, to get everything tended. Law students. I would've murdered to have been any of them, but, then, we hated fucking flatlanders. This was our lake, our home, even if the state park was named Potawatomi. I guiltily listened to their banter, barely understanding. "See, that's why you're torts." "It's weed out, but not *really* weed out." "Yeah, Kirkland and Ellis, go marquee if you can." "Heavy company for a cornhusker kid." Then the beer pong paused, and a guy in a sleeveless fleece vest started doing party tricks. Physics tricks.

It was all obvious stuff. Setting up a scrap of paper five feet away, then finger gunning it over like he had the force or something. (He'd rubbed his stubble to generate static electricity, then discharged it.) Putting his hand on his head and then asking the lunkheads to try to pull it off. (You'd actually have to lift someone's full body weight.) Then he grabbed a shot glass and a business card, filled the glass almost to the brim, laid the card on top, flipped it over—and the card held. The girls clapped, the other guys looked annoyed, started accusing him of using glue or something. But, of course, sleeveless vest turned the glass back over, slid the card right off, tossed down the shot, took a few mock bows while the girls clapped again.

"Pressure differential," I muttered.

Sleeveless vest's ears perked up. A few minutes later, he came over. "What'd you say?"

"Oh, it's . . . Sorry, I don't want trouble."

"No, tell me."

"It's easy. Air pressure inside the glass is lower than outside it."

"Okay, but what about gravity?"

"Gravity is nothing. A fridge magnet is enough to beat it."

"Where'd you learn that?"

I shrugged. "Fuck do you care?"

"Where'd you go?"

I knew enough not to say Sturgeon Bay High. "UW-Platteville."

"You screw up at school or something?"

"No, I got a 4.0."

"What'd you get on your SAT?"

"I . . . I don't remember."

"Never mind, how about this?" He reached for a pint glass, held it up, somewhat unsteadily. "What's greater? Its height or its circum—"

"Circumference. Pi times the radius, about nine, ten inches or so."

"Every whiz kid in here would say height."

"Yeah, but, you're lawyers."

"Angie is in law school. I'm at the Driscoll Lab. Soft matter stuff."

"Oh, like . . . liquid crystals?" I couldn't hide my excitement. "Brownian motion?"

"How old are you anyway?"

"Twenty-two," I said, lying again.

"Well, then." He fished in his pocket for the business card, now ringed from where the shot had soaked through. "Driscoll does outreach. You're ever near Northwestern, email me."

"Seattle?" I murmured. "That's kind of far . . ."

Sleeveless gave me a look like maybe I was joking.

"Sweet," I mumbled and pocketed the card.

The guy went over to talk to Angie. Mays had her in the corner. Her eyes were darting around, looking for an escape. He was talking quickly, nervously, flecks of saliva popping out of his mouth and landing on her cowgirl shirt. When sleeveless arrived, she put her arm around him, kissed him showily. My blood churned again, but not for myself.

Sleeveless started talking at Mays. I watched him squirming. Then he suddenly excused himself, went over to the ping-pong table, started playing against cargo shorts and another dude. Once, then three, four times he slapped the ball back. It whizzed past their heads, clattered off the wall. They laughed at that. But the sixth, seventh time, I could see them getting pissed. "Hey, there, guy," cargo shorts said, "let's take a break, yeah?"

"What's that smell?" the other dude put in. "There's a weird smell. Fish or something."

Abruptly, Mays thunked his paddle down on the table. The blood drained out of his face. I waited for that wordless scream. Instead, he pushed through the screen door and wandered outside. I followed him as he trudged toward his truck. Here at the end of the point, the water was all around you, lapping in from all directions at once. I was drunker than I realized, yet completely lucid. I touched the business card in my pocket, looked down the curve of the shore, at the flashes of heat lightning, and swore I could see all the way to the Sears Tower.

"*Now* you want to go?" I called ahead to Mays. "Come on, it's not so bad."

"Who are you?"

"What?"

"Who the fuck are you, assistant manager?"

"Mays, man, what are you talking about?"

He clambered up into the bed of his truck, where all those carcasses had been hauled, and started fooling with the lockbox. I thought maybe he was getting more booze. And then I saw it: a long, forest-camo bag. My gut flopped over as he pulled out the twenty-gauge, slotted two shells, and started back to the cabin.

"Fuck you, Shart. All of you."

"Mays! Jesus, Mays. I don't think we want to—"

I grabbed his arm, then came to my senses, let him shake me off, not wanting that shotgun turned on me. He pushed through the screen door. The room went silent. They just stood there clutching their drinks, jaws held tight. One guy shook his head, smiled sadly, sucked a tooth, like this was what they'd expected from us all along. Mays went right up to him.

"What'd you smell?" he said, waggling the twenty-gauge in the guy's face. "Huh? You smell something?" Then he waved the barrel under cargo shorts' nose. "Take a sniff. Good long one. Real, real slow."

"Gonna kill you," cargo shorts muttered. "Really gonna kill you."

"With what?" Mays said. "Real, real slow. Line it up, she told me. Get them in the lungs. Blam! Straight through."

"Mays . . ." I said, but no one heard me. No one even saw me, rapt as they all were by the end of that twenty-gauge. Some of the guys were big-dogging it, puffing out their chests, whispering, "You're dead, dude." A couple of others were maneuvering to the edge of the room, as if to flank Mays. But most of the room had gone blank, disappeared deep inside themselves. Only Angie was looking Mays in the eyes.

"Said I was getting out cash," she told him. "You think I haven't seen the redneck act before?"

Mays met her gaze without seeing her. "She was better than any of us. Why would she come back?" he whispered. "Minky fucking stinky."

The lighthouse beam swept over us, casting the room in shadow, showing every bead of sweat on the students' terrified, outraged faces. For maybe half a minute, we were *their* lords. Then Mays laughed, giggled like a hiccup, pressed a fist against his shiner, rubbing off the concealer, then turned and banged back out the screen door.

I hung there a minute, staring at the faces staring back at me—Angie, sleeveless vest—trying to tell them with my eyes, to make them recognize me. Finally, I ran out after Mays. We jumped into the truck, peeled out in a spray of gravel, lurched back down the winding dark road.

And though we were whooping and shouting—"Fuck! Fucking flatlanders!"—I felt the future stirring slow and heavy inside me—we'd be lucky we didn't get picked up by the cops, sent down to Kettle

Moraine—like when a tornado's coming and the sky goes all green. I thought about my pop talking about his decoys, and I understood: *He* was the lone duck swimming circles, telling me to keep on flying. I felt in my pocket for the business card, felt the charge of it, the possibility. And then I tore it to pieces, let them go, one by one, out of the window. We approached the old lighthouse, its flour-white column looming, the blinding beam endlessly sweeping back and forth, erasing the night.

"Stop here," I told Mays.

We jumped out of the pickup. "Minky stinky!" I screamed as we ran toward the lake, backlit by the beam, our shadows a hundred feet long. I grabbed the biggest rock I could, turned and hurled it up at the light, longing for the crash. And then a boom thundered through me, louder than the future, Mays with his boyhood gun, firing up at that huge delicate glass bulb. I grabbed another rock, another. We set to it. We got back to fucking work.

ACKNOWLEDGMENTS

My enduring gratitude to everyone who read, listened, and helped me along the way, especially Katie Adams, Molly Antopol, Jim Baker, Ann Beattie, Sierra Bellows, Ryan Bieber, Cara Blue Adams, Jinn Bronwen Lee, Luke Brown, Chad Burnett, Kat Carlson, John Casey, Deborah Eisenberg, Brendan Fitzgerald, Adam Foley, Tom Franklin, Aja Gabel, Javier Galindo, Marielle Gross, Gail Hochman, JAWSTORMS, Leslie Jamison, Drew Johnson, Darren Jones, Laura Kaye, Jason Labbe, Catherine Lacey, David Levine, John L'Heureux, Ling Ma, Anthony Marra, Natalie Mengel, Claire Mengel, Robin Metz, Gabe Patti, Holly Pearson, Sylvia Pearson Coonan, Valer Popa, Max Porter, Todd Portnowitz, Dan Raeburn, Alex Robinson, Tina Rodia, Augustus Rose, Erin Saldin, Caitlin Satchell, David Schutter, Brynn Seibert, Maggie Shipstead, Rob Smith, Natania Rosenfeld, Jill Smith, Stephanie Soileau, Mary Speaker, Elizabeth Tallent, Cam Terwilliger, Ted Thompson, Chris Tilghman, Janet Tozer, John Tozer, Vu Tran, Gemma Trevisani, Laura van den Berg, Gina Welch, Myung Wesner, Sarah Wetmore, John Wilkinson, Tobias Wolff, Cutter Wood, and Nina Young.

For all of their passionate, intelligent work and guidance in bringing these stories into the world, thank you to Lori Ostlund, Ivo Fravashi, Sarah Francis Fitch Shermyen, Jon Davies, and the University of Georgia Press; Jin Auh, Jessica Bullock, Abram Scharf, Alba Ziegler-Bailey, and everyone at the Wylie Agency; the BBC, BBC Radio 4, Mark Strong, Liz Allard, Gemma Jenkins, and Rowan Routh; the Comma Press; Oscar Villalon, Manjula Martin, Laura Cogan, Tom Jenks, Sudip

Bose, Robert Wilson, Luke Neima, Paul Reyes, Allison Wright, and the other brilliant magazine editors with whom I've been privileged to collaborate.

My deepest thanks, too, for the generous support of these institutions and individuals: the American Academy of Arts and Letters, the American Academy in Rome, the John Guare Writer's Fund, Dorothy and Lewis B. Cullman, Michael Collier, Noreen Cargill, the Bread Loaf Writers' Conference, Martin Pick, the Charles Pick Fellowship, the University of East Anglia, Stanford University, the Truman Capote Literary Trust, MacDowell, Yaddo, Anne Sikora, Art Omi, the Virginia Center for the Creative Arts, and the University of Chicago and Royal Holloway, University of London, and my pals and colleagues at both.

Finally, I want to acknowledge the support and love of my friends and family. I'll never be able to thank you enough.

THE FLANNERY O'CONNOR AWARD FOR SHORT FICTION

David Walton, *Evening Out*
Leigh Allison Wilson, *From the Bottom Up*
Sandra Thompson, *Close-Ups*
Susan Neville, *The Invention of Flight*
Mary Hood, *How Far She Went*
François Camoin, *Why Men Are Afraid of Women*
Molly Giles, *Rough Translations*
Daniel Curley, *Living with Snakes*
Peter Meinke, *The Piano Tuner*
Tony Ardizzone, *The Evening News*
Salvatore La Puma, *The Boys of Bensonhurst*
Melissa Pritchard, *Spirit Seizures*
Philip F. Deaver, *Silent Retreats*
Gail Galloway Adams, *The Purchase of Order*
Carole L. Glickfeld, *Useful Gifts*
Antonya Nelson, *The Expendables*
Nancy Zafris, *The People I Know*
Robert Abel, *Ghost Traps*
T. M. McNally, *Low Flying Aircraft*
Alfred DePew, *The Melancholy of Departure*
Dennis Hathaway, *The Consequences of Desire*
Rita Ciresi, *Mother Rocket*
Dianne Nelson Oberhansly, *A Brief History of Male Nudes in America*
Christopher McIlroy, *All My Relations*
Carol Lee Lorenzo, *Nervous Dancer*
C. M. Mayo, *Sky over El Nido*

Wendy Brenner, *Large Animals in Everyday Life*
Paul Rawlins, *No Lie Like Love*
Harvey Grossinger, *The Quarry*
Ha Jin, *Under the Red Flag*
Andy Plattner, *Winter Money*
Frank Soos, *Unified Field Theory*
Mary Clyde, *Survival Rates*
Hester Kaplan, *The Edge of Marriage*
Darrell Spencer, *CAUTION Men in Trees*
Robert Anderson, *Ice Age*
Bill Roorbach, *Big Bend*
Dana Johnson, *Break Any Woman Down*
Gina Ochsner, *The Necessary Grace to Fall*
Kellie Wells, *Compression Scars*
Eric Shade, *Eyesores*
Catherine Brady, *Curled in the Bed of Love*
Ed Allen, *Ate It Anyway*
Gary Fincke, *Sorry I Worried You*
Barbara Sutton, *The Send-Away Girl*
David Crouse, *Copy Cats*
Randy F. Nelson, *The Imaginary Lives of Mechanical Men*
Greg Downs, *Spit Baths*
Peter LaSalle, *Tell Borges If You See Him: Tales of Contemporary Somnambulism*
Anne Panning, *Super America*
Margot Singer, *The Pale of Settlement*
Andrew Porter, *The Theory of Light and Matter*
Peter Selgin, *Drowning Lessons*
Geoffrey Becker, *Black Elvis*
Lori Ostlund, *The Bigness of the World*
Linda LeGarde Grover, *The Dance Boots*
Jessica Treadway, *Please Come Back to Me*
Amina Gautier, *At-Risk*
Melinda Moustakis, *Bear Down, Bear North*
E. J. Levy, *Love, in Theory*
Hugh Sheehy, *The Invisibles*
Jacquelin Gorman, *The Viewing Room*
Tom Kealey, *Thieves I've Known*

Karin Lin-Greenberg, *Faulty Predictions*
Monica McFawn, *Bright Shards of Someplace Else*
Toni Graham, *The Suicide Club*
Siamak Vossoughi, *Better Than War*
Lisa Graley, *The Current That Carries*
Anne Raeff, *The Jungle Around Us*
Becky Mandelbaum, *Bad Kansas*
Kirsten Sundberg Lunstrum, *What We Do with the Wreckage*
Colette Sartor, *Once Removed*
Patrick Earl Ryan, *If We Were Electric*
Kate McIntyre, *Mad Prairie*
Toni Ann Johnson, *Light Skin Gone to Waste*
Carol Roh Spaulding, *Waiting for Mr. Kim and Other Stories*
Iheoma Nwachukwu, *Japa and Other Stories*
A. Muia, *A Desert between Two Seas*
Will Boast, *The Submerged*

Anniversary Anthologies

TENTH ANNIVERSARY
The Flannery O'Connor Award: Selected Stories, edited by Charles East

FIFTEENTH ANNIVERSARY
Listening to the Voices: Stories from the Flannery O'Connor Award, edited by Charles East

THIRTIETH ANNIVERSARY
Stories from the Flannery O'Connor Award: A 30th Anniversary Anthology: The Early Years, edited by Charles East
Stories from the Flannery O'Connor Award: A 30th Anniversary Anthology: The Recent Years, edited by Nancy Zafris

Thematic Anthologies

Hold That Knowledge: Stories about Love from the Flannery O'Connor Award for Short Fiction, edited by Ethan Laughman
The Slow Release: Stories about Death from the Flannery O'Connor Award for Short Fiction, edited by Ethan Laughman

Spinning Away from the Center: Stories about Homesickness and Homecoming from the Flannery O'Connor Award for Short Fiction, edited by Ethan Laughman

Rituals to Observe: Stories about Holidays from the Flannery O'Connor Award for Short Fiction, edited by Ethan Laughman

Good and Balanced: Stories about Sports from the Flannery O'Connor Award for Short Fiction, edited by Ethan Laughman

Down on the Sidewalk: Stories about Children and Childhood from the Flannery O'Connor Award for Short Fiction, edited by Ethan Laughman

A Perfect Souvenir: Stories about Travel from the Flannery O'Connor Award for Short Fiction, edited by Ethan Laughman

A Day's Pay: Stories about Work from the Flannery O'Connor Award for Short Fiction, edited by Ethan Laughman

Growing Up: Stories about Adolescence from the Flannery O'Connor Award for Short Fiction, edited by Ethan Laughman

Changes: Stories about Transformation from the Flannery O'Connor Award for Short Fiction, edited by Ethan Laughman